Pri

Hell's Ankho

Aiden Bates & Ali Lyda

© 2021

Disclaimer

This is a work of fiction. Names, places, characters, and events are all fictitious for the reader's pleasure. Any similarities to real people, places, events, living or dead are all coincidental.

Contents

Chapter 1 - Mal

I was having a good dream—a *really* good dream. It was a familiar dream by now, too—I was in a huge bed, with silky-soft sheets, supine beneath a gorgeously muscled man. I wasn't supine for long, though. I wrapped my legs around us and flipped us over, so he was beneath me, pinned facedown to sheets, and both of us laughed at the sudden change in position. He wrestled against my hold, his muscles straining beautifully. Then he made a low noise, like a growl, and flipped us again so that I was on the bottom.

The easy way he manipulated my body sent a rush of heat through me. I loved this part of the dream, loved a man who could match my strength and overpower me, who wasn't afraid of a little roughhousing to get into the mood.

The man above me laughed, low and warm and familiar, as he straddled my hips. He wrapped one big, callused hand around my wrists, pinning them over my head. I arched and thrashed beneath him, testing his strength, and he didn't budge an inch. The sensation of pushing against his hold and *failing* turned me on so fucking much.

Now that I was pinned beneath him, my desire was only heightened. Familiar blue eyes locked on mine before he claimed my mouth, his salt and pepper beard a delicious scratch against my skin. I loved it when Priest held me down like this and pressed the hard length of his huge cock against me—I couldn't wait to feel him inside me.

Wait.

I woke up like I'd been electrocuted and sat up straight in bed.

Wait, *Priest*?!

My cock was painfully hard, and I cursed to myself, throat scratchy with sleep, as I shook off the vestiges of the dream. I'd been dreaming about this anonymous man for months: the same broad barrel chest, same salt-and-pepper chest hair, same thick thighs and muscular, square ass. The dreams had been pretty similar every time I'd had them, rolling around in a bed big enough that there was no risk of rolling off the edge, with the same faceless guy wrestling me for dominance.

I loved a little playful competition during sex, and the guy in the dreams was a perfect match—sometimes I won, sometimes he did, but regardless of who won, I woke up with a mess in my sheets like I was a teenager.

The guy had always been faceless. Until now.

I should've known.

I'd thought I was just nebulously horny lately, and that my brain had invented a guy who was exactly my type to just let off some steam. But of course, nothing could be that easy. And now, it seemed obvious—those familiar shoulders, the scratch of the beard even when he was faceless in my dream.

With a heaving sigh, I climbed out of bed, trying to ignore the heavy weight of my hard cock. I stretched my arms lazily over my head as I padded into my bathroom. I lived in one of the studio apartments in the Hell's Ankhor Crew

Junee clubhouse—it was just the right size for me, with a king-sized bed separated from the rest of the room by a dressing screen, a kitchenette and a recently remodeled bathroom on the other side.

Perks of being the president meant I got one of the nicest studios in the building. It had everything I needed and then some—and yet, recently I'd begun to feel a little itchy in the space, like something was missing. I couldn't quite put my finger on what it was, though. Likely I just needed to move my furniture around or get a new piece of art. Something to freshen up the space. I'd lived here for quite some time now, and maybe I was due for a change.

I turned the water on in the shower as hot as I could stand it and climbed under the spray. The water thrummed against my back, soothing some of the tension from the dream, and I closed my eyes.

Of course, my thoughts immediately drifted back to Priest.

I'd known Priest for over thirty years now. *Jeez*. Those kinds of numbers still didn't feel real, but that was the reality of aging, I guessed. We'd met in our twenties, and as soon as I'd met him, I'd thought he was gorgeous with his keen blue eyes, short beard, and broad shoulders. And he carried himself with a wisdom beyond his years, even when he was young. But when we'd met, he'd already been in love with one of my oldest friends—Aaron, who took the handle Ankh. And despite how hot I thought Priest was, they were so clearly happy together I didn't have the slightest desire to mess with that.

I'd known Aaron growing up, but we'd lost touch when he moved out to Los Angeles for school. When he'd returned to Elkin Lake, it was with Priest on his arm and a new burning desire to start Hell's Ankhor. I was so fucking happy for them both—they fit each other the way a bike chain fits on the teeth of the cog. A perfect balance. I was already part of the Liberty Crew at the time, but not in the inner circle yet, and I was thrilled that there was going to be another club nearby.

Growing our clubs side by side was one of the greatest joys of my life. I'd leaned on them a lot as I'd grown into a leadership role within the Liberty Crew, always asking for advice or guidance or just a place to vent about club issues to people who really understood. We spent a lot of time together—Priest and Ankh became like uncles to Dante and Tru as they grew up.

When we lost Ankh a few years ago, there were moments I thought we might lose Priest, too. His grief had swallowed him. He spent days in bed, hardly ate. He was a shell of a man for a long time. It was only his club, and his son, who were eventually able to drag him out of the darkest depths, and slowly help him recover and heal.

Watching the brightness and the openness return to Priest had been a joy and a relief, and I knew watching his brothers-in-arms find love had been no small part of that. He'd never be the man he was before Ankh was killed, but he was becoming someone just as kind and strong and wise—and handsome.

I sighed and placed one hand on the cool tile of the shower, focusing on the heat of the water and the warm steam as I breathed in. I just couldn't believe that I was having *sex dreams* about one of my oldest friends. I'd always found him handsome, and as he aged, he was only getting more attractive: with silver streaks in his dark hair, crow's feet and laugh lines, and a new layer of softness over his strong body.

Fuck. My cock was still hard from the dream, from the way dream-Priest had laughed warmly as he'd held me down and grinded his dick against my ass. I felt a little slimy, but I couldn't help it—there was no way I was going to get through my day if I didn't at least take the edge off. I was just taking care of physical needs here. It didn't have to be anything weird.

I gripped my cock and it throbbed in my hand. I groaned in relief at the sensation; I felt like I was already teetering on the edge, like the dream had gotten me almost all the way there. The shower had done nothing to ease my near-painful arousal. I couldn't help but relive the dream as I jerked off rough and fast: the sensation of Priest's muscular body pinning me down, his hands on my wrists, his beard scratching across my skin. It felt good—really good—but I was still rushing it, jerking myself efficiently, like if I got it over quickly, it'd be less terrible that I was jerking off to thoughts of Priest. Even if they were dream thoughts.

I came with a low moan, savoring the rush of relief that accompanied it. My muscles tensed and relaxed, and I finally felt like I could breathe again.

Yeah, the orgasm had cleared my head, thank God. I pushed away the lingering sense of guilt as I finished showering, then got dressed in a hurry and made my way downstairs, where the clubhouse was in the throes of morning chaos as usual.

Dante was manning the kitchen, making mountains of eggs and toast, with Heath hanging off him and distracting him with teasing kisses. Eli and Star were hovering over a laptop, looking at the enforcement schedule, and the schedule for Stella's as well. Tru was on the couch with a cup of coffee, his feet kicked in Beau's lap as Beau flipped through television channels.

"Morning, folks," I hollered as I descended the stairs. "Is there coffee?"

"Of course there's coffee," Star said, without looking up. "How long have you lived here?"

"Way too long," I said with a grin.

Dante passed the spatula to Heath so Heath could babysit the immense pan of eggs, and then poured me a coffee. He handed it over with a smile. "Here ya go, Dad."

"What's the occasion?" I asked, raising my eyebrows at the breakfast spread.

"Just felt like it," Dante said with a shrug. "Can't a man treat his club?"

"No complaints here," I said, leaning against the counter with my coffee in hand. As I watched the morning hustle and bustle around me, I was struck, as I often was, with a sudden burst of gratitude. I was so lucky to have these people in my corner. My foundation.

My phone buzzed in my jeans pocket. I expected something from one of the Elkin Lake guys—we had a church meeting planned today, just for the presidents and vices, but we hadn't worked out the details yet. But the number on my lock screen immediately made my mood sour.

It was an unfamiliar number, but the content of the message – *good morning, gorgeous, I miss you, when can I see you* – made it obvious who it was. Stefan. No matter how many times I blocked him, he'd end up with a new number and get right back to texting me like nothing had happened. He was constantly calling and texting, even though I never responded. I hardly even knew the guy! I'd made the mistake of hooking up with him at Stallions months ago, and he hadn't left me alone since.

"Who is it?" Dante asked, peering curiously at me.

I realized then I was glaring at my phone like I wanted to set it alight. Instead, I just closed the message and stuffed my phone back into my pocket.

"It's nothing," I said. "How are those eggs coming along? I'm hungry!"

Dante recognized the deflection for what it was; he gave me a sideways glance but let it slide. The guys were starting to get suspicious, though. They'd noticed how often my phone was buzzing, and I wasn't great about hiding my reaction when Stefan texted me. I was getting really fucking sick of it. But it wasn't anything more than an annoyance—eventually he'd get sick of my lack of reaction and move on. So far, though, no matter how much I iced him out, he just kept messaging and messaging.

Whatever. I had bigger things to worry about—such as ensuring Heath didn't burn down the Crew Motel when he inevitably forgot about the toast. And hopefully, getting back to the everyday craziness of the club would push the dream about Priest from my mind.

Chapter 2 - Priest

I leaned against my granite counter as the percolator bubbled on the gas stove, a familiar, quiet sound that always soothed me. The warm morning sun slanted into my cabin, setting the room aglow. I always woke up early, and today was no different. When I was living in the clubhouse, the early morning was often my only cherished moment of solace before the rest of the club members woke up and began filling the clubhouse with their cheerful noise. Now, though, I could take as much time in the kitchen as I wanted, starting my day slowly before I strolled over to the clubhouse to join the chaos.

I gazed out the back window, over the narrow back porch and across the undeveloped Hell's Ankhor Crew land. It was a gorgeous, quiet morning, and I opened the window to let the chilly morning air in, and to hear the familiar chirping of the birds outside.

After Ankh had passed, I'd thought I'd never find happiness again. And yet, somehow, as time had gone by and my brothers had helped me heal, I'd found something almost like contentment again. I had Ankhor Works, and now Stella's; the growth of the club meant we had a nearly unshakeable foundation, and of course I had my son, Raven.

But.

There was always a but, wasn't there?

I sighed and turned away from the window as the percolator finished brewing the coffee. I couldn't deny the twinge of loneliness in my chest as I puttered around the cabin.

With a mug of coffee in hand, I leaned against the counter and sighed, gazing at the fridge. The door of the fancy stainless steel appliance was already nearly covered in photos—Jonah and Raven had gathered pictures from all the members, plastering them on the fridge before I moved in. The photos were a retrospective of the club, from its foundation to the construction of the cabin itself: pictures of birthdays, parties, cookouts, the opening of Ankhor Works, the opening of Stella's, baby pictures of Raven, and now of Grace.

And, of course, photos of Ankh.

There was a copy of one of my favorite photos, too, of Ankh and me standing outside Ballast when we'd first opened it, with our arms slung around each other, both mid-laugh. Like we couldn't contain our joy. That's how we'd felt, too—I remembered it vividly. Opening Ballast had been a dream come true.

God, I missed his laugh.

The twinge of loneliness crawled into my throat and tightened into a knot. I pulled the photo off the fridge and smoothed my thumb over the edge.

"What am I supposed to do now?" I asked the photo. "God, Ankh. I miss you so much." I laughed a little to myself as I rubbed at my eyes, suddenly prickling with familiar tears. "I'm doing—doing as well as I can be without you, but God, I could really use your advice."

I missed his voice, his smile, his embrace. And moments like this, when I felt lost or confused, were when I missed him the most. My brothers-in-arms in the club seemed to think that I was the one with all the answers these days—and I was happy to help them whenever I could. But I lacked the same drive Ankh had, that inner fire that pushed the club forward. That same fire Blade had.

I did the best I could, and I tried to live up to the way the members talked about me—*the heart of the club*, it still made me smile to remember it—but I didn't have *all* the answers. Ankh had always been my partner in moments like this, and we'd work together to find solutions, or just untangle my confusing emotions.

He'd been my home for more than half my life. And now this cabin, as gorgeous as it was, felt like something was missing.

But this was just part of the grieving process. I had moments like this—whole days like it, too. Some days were just harder than others. And today, despite the pang of grief, was still better than lots of other days I'd had before.

I cleared my throat and put the photo back on the fridge. I knew one thing Ankh would tell me now—to stop moping alone at home and go lean on the rest of the club. If there was a guaranteed way to boost my mood, it was a little bit of early morning chaos at the clubhouse.

I finished my coffee, then strolled down the short path between the cabin and the clubhouse. Even though it was still early, a handful of members were awake and starting their day in the big kitchen: Raven, Jazz, and Joker were all up and, thankfully, quiet.

"Morning, Priest," Joker said brightly. "Had your coffee already?"

"Of course," I said. "Wouldn't say no to another cup, though."

Which was why we had the industrial-sized coffeemaker in the clubhouse. Joker nodded knowingly and poured me a cup.

"How's the new place, Pop?" Raven asked from where he was booting up his laptop at the big communal table.

Despite the early hour, he looked especially bright-eyed, blue eyes gleaming. Maybe it was because I was already primed to ache today, but he looked so much like Ankh, it made my heart hurt. Mostly knowing that Ankh would be so proud of how he'd grown up, and what an important role he'd taken on in the club.

"It's amazing," I said. "I sleep like a baby, finally." I shot a smirk at Jazz. "No noisy neighbors keeping me up."

"What!" Jazz said, faux-scandalized with a hand on his chest. "And with all the money I spent on that gag—"

"Too early," Raven interrupted. "Let me have another coffee before you start with the ball gag jokes."

"I never said ball gag," Jazz noted.

"I'm interested in hearing more, actually," Joker teased.

I rolled my eyes fondly. That *was* a major benefit of having the cabin, though—no more waking up to the telltale signs of a bedframe knocking against the wall on both sides. As happy as I was that the members were finding love, it had started making me feel a little like I was living in a frat house.

"Put it in the minutes for the next church meeting," I said. "Club funds to spend on ball gags."

Joker barked a laugh, and Jazz grinned as well. "For today's meeting?" Jazz asked. "Thought that was head honchos only."

"Only the most important business," I agreed seriously, which set Joker laughing again.

"Guys!" Raven said with a shake of his head. "Pop, for *real*, how's the cabin?"

And he looked a little concerned, like he thought I was deflecting something with the jokes. Coffee in hand, I sidled up to Raven and swung my arm around his shoulder. He sighed, leaning against me as he pulled up the financial spreadsheets I'd asked him to prepare for the church meeting.

"It's great," I said, my voice a little lower. Jazz and Joker were busy in the kitchen now, rooting around for an easy breakfast like high schoolers in a rush. I sighed and admitted, "But it feels like something's missing. I haven't quite put my finger on it yet. I think I just need to get used to the quiet."

Raven pressed his lips together, visibly turning that sentence over in his mind as his hands hovered over the keyboard. Of course he couldn't just let the comment slide—he was like his dad. Probably trying to figure out what I meant, and what he could do to fix it.

I was so blessed to have Raven here, in the club. He was so smart—he could've gone anywhere with his skills, and he chose to stay here with his family. Still trying to take care of me, even though *I* was the parent. I ruffled his hair like I used to do back when he was a kid.

"Pop," Raven said with a huffed sigh. "Quit it."

"Can't help it, kid," I said. "You look so much like your dad."

Raven's expression softened.

"He'd be really proud of you," I said, my voice valiantly steady around the tightness in my chest. "Now come on, send me that spreadsheet so I have time to review it before church."

"Morning," Gunnar boomed as he hustled down the stairs, his hair still damp from his shower.

Raven rubbed briskly at his eyes. "Hey, there's coffee."

Gunnar furrowed his eyebrows at Raven, then at me. I stepped away with a small smile, and Gunnar swooped in and wound his arms around Raven's shoulders from behind him, then dropped a kiss to Raven's temple.

"Spreadsheets that bad?" he teased gently.

"Yes," Raven said with a pout, but it broke quickly into a smile. "They're awful."

I knew later that night, Raven and Gunnar would be debriefing our conversation, and Raven would be trying to figure out how he could improve the cabin. Or just what I meant. The thought warmed me, honestly, even though I didn't *want* Raven to worry. Raven had a tendency to get trapped in looping, anxious thoughts, especially about things he couldn't control. But now, much to my relief, he had Gunnar to break him out of those spirals. They were such a perfect fit. I'd had my hesitations when they'd first started to circle each other, but once Gunnar had gotten his head out of his ass, it was clear they were meant to be together.

"Hey, guys," Heath said with a smile as he shouldered the door open. He was laden down with boxes from Stella's. "Dante's on his way in a bit, he's just wrapping up some prep, but he wanted me to bring these over for y'all and for the meeting. He said he and Mal would be over in a couple hours."

I glanced up at the sound of Mal's name, like Gretel when she heard the word 'treat.' Then I immediately flushed with embarrassment, even though no one had noticed the way I looked up.

It was ridiculous, the effect just hearing Mal's name had on me. Being around Mal always boosted my mood—he had such a warm, comfortable presence—and recently, I'd started to look forward more and more to the time we got to spend together. The comfort I felt around him had slowly been transforming into something warm and unexpected curling in my gut. Something that felt a lot like desire.

I wasn't ready to tackle that feeling yet, though. How could I want someone else when I still missed Ankh so badly? Of course, I knew Ankh would want me to move on and be happy, but it didn't feel right—not yet, at least. And wanting Mal in this way felt like I was taking advantage of his friendship. How could I know I wanted Mal for *Mal*, and not just because he'd been a pillar of strength for me throughout my grief? It was all so tangled up—grief, guilt, loss, gratitude, and desire.

The confusion only made me miss Ankh anew.

I took a steadying breath and refocused on the present, and the current descent of club members onto the box of scones on the table. Right now, I had to focus on the upcoming church meeting, and being the vice president, this club needed to me.

Raven appeared at my side and pushed a scone into my hands. "Everything okay?" he asked, chin ducked with concern.

I took the scone with a smile of thanks and nodded. "Everything's great."

The last thing I wanted was for Raven to worry. And it wasn't a lie. Ankh would be proud of the club—proud of us all.

Whatever I felt for Mal, I'd figure it out, the same way I'd gotten through these past few years: one day at a time.

Chapter 3 - Mal

I gunned my engine, relishing the rush of the wind in my ears and the rumble of the bike beneath me. It was only twenty minutes from Junee to Elkin Lake, but what a glorious twenty minutes it was—the winding highway, the chilly air, the distinct lack of speed-checking police.

It'd rained the night previous, which meant the road was a little slick with water, requiring a bit more attention than usual. I loved that about riding, how I had to adjust how I handled my bike to match the conditions of the road. It made me feel connected to my bike, and to the asphalt beneath me. Getting into that Zen flow state of riding was something I cherished.

I was so focused on the road ahead, though, that I didn't notice the shallow puddle right in front of me until it was too close to swerve. It wasn't dangerous, but—ugh! I grimaced as my bike cut through the water and kicked up mud all over my riding leathers and the usually spotless body of my bike.

But that was fine. It hadn't been a *huge* puddle—it'd be fairly easy to clean off after church, and I wasn't *too* wet.

Then, as if on cue in a slapstick comedy, a trunk gunned its engine behind me and sped up to pass me. As it did, it ran through another shallow puddle, drenching me in a terrible arc of gross gray rainwater. I swore loudly but kept my bike steady as the truck barreled by and roared down the highway.

My good mood soured as I finished up the drive to the Elkin Lake clubhouse. When I arrived, I was thoroughly drenched and cold, the denim of my pants sticking heavily to my legs, my leather jacket coated in a thin layer of mud. I dismounted, pulled off my helmet, and cringed at the state of my bike.

"Oh, no," I whined to myself. "Baby, I'm so sorry." I pulled a soft rag out of my saddlebag, stashed there specifically for this purpose, and began to hurriedly wipe down the body of the bike before the dirt dried and got too caked on. "You know I didn't mean for this to happen."

A low laugh caught my attention—and caused a familiar curl of heat to unspool in my gut.

I straightened up and watched as Priest ambled down the stairs, one hand in the pocket of his leather jacket and the other around a mug of coffee. He moved with an easy, leonine grace, and a warm smile curved on his lips as he approached me.

"The way you talk to that bike, I'd think you loved it more than your firstborn," he said.

"More than Dante?" I said with a grin as I wiped my hands off on the towel. "Hmm, it's close, but I think he pulls ahead."

Priest laughed again, and there was that damn curl of heat again. It was so easy to talk to him, and be around him, but—this physical reaction to his presence was new. Maybe it was the dream; it'd heightened my reactions and put me on edge. Luckily, it wasn't enough to make me *act* any differently around him, even if I *felt* differently. Even if I wanted to step closer, hear that laugh again right in my ear, feel that beard scratch across my skin.

I blinked hard and shook away the remnants of the dream, just as quickly as they bubbled to the surface. I turned my attention back to the bike instead. "A man can't take care of his bike? Might be second to Dante, but it's definitely the longest relationship I've ever had."

Priest snorted. "*You're* soaked, too—not just the bike."

"I know." I grimaced, trying to ignore the extremely uncomfortable way my wet jeans were sticking to my legs. "Some dumbass in a truck passed me on the highway and of course went through a huge puddle as he did."

"Just your luck," Priest said with a shake of his head. "Blade and Dante are still setting up inside. Come on, you can borrow some dry clothes. No point in having a meeting if you're just going to be sitting around miserable in your wet jeans."

"Can't argue with that," I said. I was already starting to shiver, with my wet clothes and the chilly air, so I followed Priest down the path to his cabin.

I'd been inside the cabin a few times, and every time I visited, it felt homier and homier. I left my leather jacket draped over the porch rail outside, then toed off my muddy boots into his stack of shoes.

"It'll be just a second," Priest said as he hurried into his lofted bedroom. Mindful not to drip on the carpet, I padded into the kitchen, drawn to the photos covering the doors of the stainless-steel fridge. One in the center caught my eye—a young Aaron and Priest, arms around each other's shoulders in front of Ballast.

God, they both looked so young. And so happy. Hard to believe how much time had passed—hard to believe we'd ever been that young.

"I was looking at that same picture this morning," Priest said as he descended the stairs with a shirt and sweatpants in hand.

"Aaron's so handsome here," I said. "And you're not half-bad yourself."

Priest huffed a little laugh. "That's right," he said. "Easy to forget you knew Ankh when he was Aaron, first."

"Yeah. To this day I think of him as Aaron just as much as I think of him as Ankh. Those years we had growing up... they were really formative for me."

A soft, thoughtful look crossed Priest's features. "I never heard a lot about those years, if I'm honest."

"I'll tell you some stories," I said. "When we're not late for a church meeting. And I still need to change."

The thoughtful look quickly became one of slight alarm. "Oh, yeah, and those boys take their punctuality seriously," Priest said. "We better get our asses moving."

With a grateful smile, I took the clothes from Priest's hands and hurried into the downstairs half-bathroom to change. I shucked off my wet jeans in a hurry, replacing them with the sweatpants, which were threadbare and super-soft with years of wear. Had Priest worn them a lot? Maybe fresh from the shower, pulling them on in his bedroom before he crawled leisurely into his bed?

I took a deep breath and tried not to think about my cock pressing against the same fabric his had countless times before. I felt like a young man, willing my cock not to get hard as I forcibly pushed the thoughts from my mind. Then I tugged off my t-shirt, grimacing as the wet collar dragged over my face, and unfolded the one Priest had given to me.

And, yeah, this wasn't going to work. It was *tiny.* Definitely wouldn't fit Priest, though the image of him trying to struggle into it did make me grin a little.

I left my shirt draped over the counter and stepped back out into the living room with the tiny shirt in hand. "Hey, Priest, I don't think this shirt is going to work, unless you want me to show up to church looking like a Spice Girl in a crop top…"

Priest turned around from where he was waiting in the kitchen.

I held up the shirt demonstratively. "See what I mean?"

Priest glanced at the shirt, but his gaze quickly turned to me instead, skittering over my chest. He swallowed visibly, then blinked and dragged his gaze with some force back to meet mine.

I flushed under the weight of his blue eyes. Suddenly I felt self-conscious, standing in the doorway shirtless, and my cheeks heated. I wasn't out of shape, by any means: there was still good definition in my pecs, and I had a strong core beneath a soft layer around my middle. I was sturdy, functional, in good shape.

I wasn't bad-looking, but I hadn't had anyone look at me like this in a hell of a long time. I wasn't used to being looked at all.

I raised my eyebrows. "Maybe I'd wear it if I were a younger man, you know, but as co-president..."

That seemed to snap Priest out of whatever odd daze he was in, and he blinked a few times. He didn't laugh at either of my little jokes, instead just swallowed again, and shifted his weight a little on his feet.

Suddenly the tension felt heavy between us, like a physical weight. It wasn't quite awkward—it was *heated*.

And that shocked me.

Priest was looking at me with *interest*. With *desire*.

The realization had me pinned to the spot. Frozen. How was I supposed to react to this? What was I supposed to do? Regardless of what strange feelings I was beginning to have for Priest, he was one of my closest friends, and we had to work together in order to keep this club moving forward. It's not like we could act on this strange tension here. I didn't even know if I should mention it. Plus, Priest was still grieving Ankh—what kind of asshole would I be if I tried to make a move when he was still hurting? I was used to one-night stands, blowing off steam. Priest wasn't someone I could sleep with and never see again.

Luckily, I didn't have to decide how to react. Before I could, Priest turned on his heel and hurried back upstairs to his bedroom.

"Sorry," he called over his shoulder. "Must be one of Raven's mixed up in my laundry."

Moments later, he tossed an Ankhor Works shirt at me, and I caught it with my face then hurried back into the bathroom.

Before I pulled it on, though, I splashed my face with cold water and took a deep, steadying breath. Whatever had just happened between us, Priest obviously didn't want to address it. And that was fine with me—it certainly made things simpler.

I pulled the shirt on over my head. It smelled homey and comforting, like laundry detergent and a hint of leather from being worn under a jacket for years and years. Then I squared my shoulders and nodded to myself in the mirror.

That odd little moment wasn't going to change anything between us. I would follow Priest's lead—and if I knew Priest, he'd put the club first.

I ignored the small pang of disappointment that thought inspired.

Chapter 4 - Priest

It was a damn good thing I wasn't the one leading this meeting.

I was seated at the kitchen island with Blade, Dante, and Mal, and we all had our laptops opened to copies of Raven's financial spreadsheet. It was an important meeting, if dull—making sure all the bills were paid, the coffers had enough padding, the leases renewed, and the goals for next year set. I was really trying to pay attention, but wrangling my attention right then felt like trying to catch a particularly feisty fish who kept breaking away from the hook.

It definitely didn't help that Mal was seated next to me, his attention focused on his laptop, his biceps straining at the sleeves of one of my old t-shirts, his thighs strong under the fabric of my sweatpants.

I couldn't stop thinking about how he'd looked stepping out of my bathroom, with Raven's shirt draped in his hands. My sweatpants had been low on his hips, and all that gorgeous dark skin had been on display, inked with faded designs winding across his shoulders and over his muscled chest. He had slight definition on his torso— broad, functional strength, not youthful gym rat strength. Seeing his muscles shift as he'd held up the shirt had made arousal burn in my gut. Shockingly sudden and hot.

The kind of desire I'd given up on feeling ever again.

It had to be the result of my new itching loneliness in the cabin—and it probably didn't help that I hadn't had any sex in over two years. I hadn't been with *anyone* since Ankh. Hadn't wanted to. I was beyond the stage in my life where I wanted hookups, and that kind of physical comfort was the last thing I wanted when I was grieving. I didn't want anyone except Ankh—didn't want anyone at all.

Ankh was the first serious relationship I'd ever had, and the only man I'd ever made love to. How was I supposed to even imagine wanting anyone else? Especially at my age?

In the past few months, though, my sex drive had started to return. Not anything crazy—I wasn't running down to Stallions for hookups—but I'd started to feel some nebulous desire again. Like my body was thawing out from the icy throes of grief.

That felt like a betrayal. Not that I'd ever act on it. The thought of being with someone new wasn't just strange, it was daunting. After only being with Ankh for so long, building something new felt so difficult, it might as well be impossible.

It still did, even more so now with Mal at my side, and my hands itching to touch him—just a hand on his shoulder or across the broad width of his back. There was an odd disconnect inside me, like my body wanted touch and connection, but my heart felt like it was too soon. Like I still shouldn't want anyone but Ankh.

Ankh wouldn't *want* me to feel that way, of course. I knew that without a doubt. He'd want me to go out and get laid and be happy. That was always what he prioritized—the happiness of the people he loved. He'd hate to see me like this, lonely and doubting myself. Yet I couldn't change the way I felt.

So I wasn't going to do anything about the way I felt about Mal. Regardless of the way I wanted to touch him, the way I wanted to see him shirtless again, the way my clothes fit his body so well, the way I couldn't get him out of my head—

"Priest!" Blade said a little sharply, in a tone that suggested it wasn't his first time calling for my attention.

I cringed. "Sorry, uh, what line item are we discussing?"

"We've moved on to the potential prospects," Blade clarified, with his eyebrows raised in such a way that I knew he'd be ragging on me for being distracted later. "You've got the information on"—Blade peered at his notes—"Xavier?"

Right, the prospects. As the club had grown, more and more people had expressed interest in joining—which was great, and it meant we got to be a little pickier with who we let in.

"Yeah," I said. "Xavier approached me at Ballast a few weeks ago, expressing interest in prospecting."

"Does he hang around Ballast a lot?" Dante asked. "A familiar face?"

"Nope," I said. "He's from up north, near Monterey, but looking for a change of scenery."

"So why us?" Blade asked. "He's willing to relocate for the club?"

"Not just willing," I said. "He *wants* to. He'd heard about the Crew's reputation for inclusivity, which is why he's interested in prospecting."

"What do you mean by that?" Mal asked.

"He's thirty—"

"Little old for a new prospect," Dante cut in.

"No age limits," Mal said firmly. "Could use some prospects with a little more life experience, anyway."

Dante shrugged in tentative agreement.

"He's thirty," I started again, after a grateful nod to Mal. Dealing with whatever I felt for him would be a lot easier if he would stop doing things like that—jumping in and reading my mind. "But he just came out to his family as gay. He's got a good career at a marketing firm, so he's not in any immediate danger of being on the streets without our resources, but his family basically disowned him."

"Shit," Blade said with a cringe.

"He's looking for a family," Mal said knowingly.

"Right," I said. "Somewhere he can feel supported."

Dante nodded. "Does he know his way around bikes?"

"Yep," I said. "Rides a Triumph. Plus, we can probably tap his marketing experience for both Ankhor Works and

Brennan's construction work. Maybe even Joker's carvings."

Blade nodded thoughtfully. "All right, and the other two, Mal?"

"Two fresh-faced high school seniors," Mal said with a grin. "They both took shop class at the local high school and fell in love with engines. One of them fixed up a busted old 1980s Honda as their final project. But they both want to apprentice at Ankhor Works, and with business picking up, it's always good to have more folks interested in learning that side of the business."

"Worker bees," Dante said with a grin. "Can't say no to that."

After a little more discussion and clarification of the vetting process—Raven had run background checks on all three and come up clean—we agreed that all three would be welcomed as prospects.

"All right," Blade said with finality. He closed his laptop with a nod. "That's it, then. We'll get the ball rolling on a welcoming party at Ballast next week."

"Sounds good to me," Mal said, and Dante and I nodded in agreement.

As the meeting adjourned, some of the odd anxiety over the moment between Mal and me earlier dissipated. Even though I'd been a little distracted, this meeting was proof that we were still able to work together. And after a good night's sleep, surely whatever went on between us today would just be another memory in the rearview.

It had to be.

Chapter 5 - Mal

Back at the Crew Motel, I hung my leather jacket up in the foyer with a cringe. It was filthy, but I'd deal with the mud on it tomorrow.

Right now, I needed to change back into my own clothes, before one of my guys saw me and ragged on me for getting splashed on the road like a rookie.

Embarrassingly, though, I really didn't want to change out of them.

Which was ridiculous. I was acting like a teenager. Worse than a teenager! Priest had only offered me a change of clothes because he was a good friend—not for any other reason. But even though I knew that, I couldn't resist tugging the neckline of the t-shirt up to my nose and inhaling deeply.

His clothes just smelled so fucking *good*. Clean fabric, leather, and maybe, if I *really* focused, a hint of Priest's warm, musky sweat. Turned out wearing his clothes turned me on a lot more than I was ready to admit.

"Enjoying that, huh?" Tru asked with laughter in his voice.

Only then did I realize I was standing at the foot of the stairs with my nose tucked into the neckline of the t-shirt. "What?" I huffed, trying to brush it off. "I'm just going upstairs to change."

"You sure?" Tru teased. "Don't wanna hang around wearing that shirt a little longer?"

My face flushed as Tru waggled his eyebrows suggestively. Tru was like a son to me, and I treasured our relationship, but he really could be a menace. He never hesitated to share what he really thought, and I knew from the wiggle of his eyebrows that I wasn't going to get out of this conversation like nothing had happened. I wasn't just the president to Tru and Dante, I was *Dad*, which meant they got special privileges to tease me relentlessly.

"Aw, come on, Dad, have a drink with us," Dante said with a grin. He'd left a little before I had, and had beaten me home.

The Crew Motel was quiet tonight—the rest of the guys were either at Ballast, or at the Elkin Lake clubhouse, as far as I could tell. Better to get this conversation over with now, when I could sate Tru's curiosity without any of the other members butting in and overhearing. With a resigned sigh, I turned around and joined them in the kitchen, where Dante was breaking out the good whiskey and pouring us each a small glass.

"So," Tru said as he swirled the whiskey in the highball glass. He hopped up onto the counter gracefully, heels knocking against the cabinet doors. "Something going on with you and Priest?"

"Not a damn thing," I said easily, and that was the truth. Even if there had been tension between us, nothing was *happening*, and nothing was going to happen. And I didn't have any intention of letting my sons know about that strange moment.

"That's a shame," Tru said with a huff. "I think you two would be cute together."

"Tru," I said warningly. "Drop it."

The last thing I needed was more encouragement for this fantasy. Because that's all it was. Better to forget it had happened at all.

"It's not really about Priest, even," Dante said. "I mean— are you seeing *anyone* these days?"

"Of course not," I said with a dismissive wave of my hand. "When would I have time to, with all the club business going on?"

"Maybe I had this dream of you sneaking off for dates or hookups," Tru said dreamily. "Everyone needs to let off some steam every now and then."

Okay, sure, maybe I'd had a hookup here or there, but that wasn't something I was super proud of, especially at my age—and not something I was willing to share with Dante and Tru. I didn't want them to dig into why I preferred hookups; it was my business, and I wasn't ready to bare my heart like that. Fact was, I'd worked hard as hell to build a stable life for myself, and for Dante, after Melanie had left us. And now, that stability was the most important thing to me. I didn't want to get wrapped up in a serious relationship only to have the rug pulled out from under me again. Hookups were all I needed, even if the club was moving away from the wild parties of our past.

"It's not a priority right now," I said. "It's not like I'm missing anything from my life." And that was true, even if sometimes it didn't *feel* true.

Dante didn't look convinced. "Come on. We all want you to be happy—to not be alone."

"I'm *not* alone," I said. "I'm less alone than ever, what with the size of the club now."

"That's not what I mean, and you know it," Dante said with a shake of his head. "You haven't been in a relationship with anyone for years. I don't think I've even seen you get *excited* about a date when they did happen. Everything was all… cursory."

"Well." I took a sip of the whiskey, savoring the warm, familiar burn. "I guess I just haven't met anyone that made me want to put in that kind of energy to getting to know someone." I thought back to the little crack I made to Priest about my longest relationship being with my bike— at the time it'd just been a joke, but now that I thought about it, it didn't feel so funny. "It has been a while, hasn't it?"

Funny how time just slips by when you're not looking.

"Yeah," Dante said. "Really has been."

"It's kind of sad, isn't it?" I asked.

Tru opened his mouth, and Dante swatted him on the thigh before he said anything. They exchanged a look that was just as plain as if Tru had said whatever was on the tip of his tongue.

"Dad, it's been thirty-four years since Mom bailed," Dante said. "Is that really still holding you back?"

"Of course not," I said, then took another sip of whiskey, savoring it so I wouldn't have to say any anything more. It was easy to say that Melanie leaving me high and dry after Dante's birth wasn't the reason I was hesitant to commit again—but I knew that it was.

Melanie and I had been high school sweethearts, and we hadn't been paragons of safe sex when we'd gotten together. We were both only nineteen when I got her pregnant, but we decided—*together*, I'd thought—to keep the baby and start our lives together as parents, despite the challenges.

But after Dante was born, Melanie had had a change of heart. As soon as she'd been discharged and we took Dante home, she packed her things and bolted. Disappeared off the face of the earth. She'd only gotten in touch to confirm that she wanted nothing to do with Dante, and she'd paid child support dutifully, and that was that. Gone.

I'd been shocked—and devastated. I'd never felt so betrayed and abandoned. I'd thought I'd known her. I'd *loved* her, and I was *excited* to start a family together with her. And then suddenly, the family was just Dante and me.

Of course, I loved him more than life itself, and throwing myself into raising him helped me get over Melanie's cut-and-run. I could even admit to myself that I'd done a pretty damn good job. Dante had grown into a hell of a man, and a hell of a vice president. But that didn't mean it had been easy to do all on my own.

Dante peered at me, still unconvinced. "Really?"

"Really," I said. "It hurt, obviously, but it was a long time ago. And I wouldn't change a thing about the way I raised you, son."

Dante sighed, unconvinced but placated. "We all just want to see you happy, you know that, right?"

"I *am* happy," I repeated. "Don't worry about an old man like me."

I hadn't met anyone in the intervening years that made me interested in opening my heart again. The feelings I had for Priest were new, certainly, but they weren't anything I could act on. And not out of any misguided sense of self-preservation, leftover from Melanie's abandonment.

No, it was because Priest was my friend—my *family.* He was a grieving widower. I hadn't desired him when he'd been with Ankh besides the recognition of his general attractiveness—I wasn't blind—and it definitely wasn't appropriate for me to want him now. There was no way I was going to put a friendship of three decades at risk because I was horny. There were other ways to take care of that.

Dante was about to say something, but my phone ringing noisily in my pocket dragged my attention away.

Maybe it was because I was already on edge from the conversation I was having with Dante and Tru, but seeing the unfamiliar number on my screen pissed me off more than it usually did. This was going from annoying to really fucking obnoxious, and I was sick of it. In a fit of frustration—and maybe with some help from the whiskey—I answered the phone, turning my back to Dante and Tru.

"Stop fucking calling," I spat into the phone. "Or I'll be paying you a visit myself."

"Oh," Stefan said at the other end of the line, his low and unfortunately familiar voice sounding surprised, like he hadn't expected me to answer. Then it dropped to something close to a purr. "Oh, Mal, I sure hope you will."

Disgust raced through me, making my stomach turn uncomfortably. Fuck, I never should've answered the phone. Now I'd fueled this asshole's chase, and his messages were only bound to increase. I hung up the phone and set it a little too firmly on the counter.

When I turned around Dante and Tru were watching me with their eyes wide. "Who was that?"

The last thing I needed was another reason for Dante and Tru to stick their noses into my business. Stefan was an irritant, but I could handle him myself. "No one," I said with an eyeroll. "Telemarketers won't leave me alone these days."

"Dad..."

"Thanks for the drink, guys," I said. "I'm really going to bed now."

I left Dante and Tru alone in the kitchen, hurrying up the stairs before they could ask any more prying questions. I could handle Stefan. I could handle the aching new feelings I had for Priest. The combination of these problems was beginning to itch, though. For so long I'd considered hookups to be the safe option—a way to keep my sex life and my home life delineated, to ensure things were stable for my club and my son.

But the ease and speed with which Stefan had chucked a wrench into my life made me nervous. Made me wonder if the hookups were worth it—or if it was time to try something new. But right now, I just needed some time alone to get my head on straight.

Chapter 6 - Priest

I leaned an elbow against the bar with a cold pint of beer in my hand. It was a chilly night, and Ballast was busy, but only with club members. We'd closed the door to civilians for the night so we could welcome our three new prospects properly. Since it was technically a special occasion, nearly all the members had turned out. It made for a warm, comforting environment, with Coop and Jazz behind the bar, Star and Gunnar enforcing, and everyone else catching up, laughing in the warmly lit space.

Nix and Dawson were here as well, both with tall, fancy mocktails that Jazz had whipped up for them. They weren't going to stay long—Nix had made that clear—but I was thrilled to see that Dawson felt comfortable enough to drop by Ballast. Maybe in the future we'd start having events like this at Stella's.

I was chatting with Mark and Paul, the two fresh-faced high school seniors looking to apprentice at Ankhor Works. Both of them had mocktails, too, substantially less fancy than Nix's and Dawson's. They were sweet kids, but they were just that—*kids*. I could hardly believe how young they looked to me. Didn't even look old enough to have a regular driver's license, let alone a motorcycle license. It made me feel old—and yet, I was glad to have that kind of youthful energy around, to keep me on my toes. Mark and Paul both seemed like the kind of high-energy, eager-to-learn guys we needed around.

Xavier was late, though. That was already a negative mark in my book—this was an important event, and showing up late, to me, demonstrated that the club wasn't a priority. He was older, though, and I knew life sometimes got in the way. I only hoped he had a good excuse, and that I hadn't wasted my time offering him a prospect position.

"So, yeah," Mark was saying, holding his drink a little nervously as he glanced around the room. "I'm hoping to go to trade school after a couple years working, to become a certified mechanic."

"And I'm thinking welding school," Paul said with a nod. "But same, neither of us really want to jump straight into more school."

"That's smart," I said. "Get some life experience under your belt before you decide what direction to go in."

"Yeah, don't do what I did," Coop said, butting into the convo as he slid Maverick, who'd just sidled up, a pint of beer. "Which is try to go straight to regular college and flunk the fuck out with a bunch of debt."

"Jeez," Paul said, cringing. "No one told you not to go?"

"They did, but…"

Then, the back door to Ballast opened, and I stopped paying attention to Coop's familiar narrative about his failed college escapades. Mal stepped inside from the back porch, with his arm swung around Blade's shoulder as he laughed uproariously at something Blade had said. It was hard to focus on anyone else in the room when Mal laughed like that, booming and unselfconscious.

He was so comfortable and confident in his riding leathers and faded leather jacket, both soft-looking from years of hard use. And he was so at ease in Ballast, untangling his arm from Blade's shoulder and greeting other members with a big grin. It was so fucking sexy—distractingly so. The gray at his temples, the crow's feet framing the corners of his dark brown eyes, his strong hands wrapped around Maverick's as he greeted him with a firm handshake— everything about the way he carried himself was lighting me up.

And what the fuck was that about? Now was not the time. This night was about our new prospects, and I needed to *focus*. I shook away the thoughts, trying to tune back into the conversation with Mark, Paul, and Coop, as Mal was quickly wrapped up into an animated conversation with Maverick.

The front door to Ballast swung open again, and Xavier finally walked in. He had white-blond hair with striking blue eyes, and a short, narrow build that belied his big personality. Walking into a place like Ballast, though, crowded with bikers, was surely intimidating—and that appeared to be the case, if the anxious way Xavier cast his gaze around the room was anything to go by. So with a friendly nod to Mark, Paul, and Coop, I hopped off my stool and strode across the room to Xavier.

"You made it," I said, clapping him on the shoulder. "Come on, there are people I need to introduce you to."

"Let's get this party started," Xavier said with a grin. Didn't apologize for being late. That irked me a little, but I'd address it later, when we could have more privacy.

I guided him over to the end of the bar, where Blade was chatting with Gunnar, Tex, and Siren. "Blade, this is Xavier, the prospect I was telling you about."

"Xavier," Blade said with a nod. "Great to meet you. Heard a lot about you."

"Thanks," Xavier said warmly, returning Blade's handshake, not looking the slightest bit intimidated now. "Really excited to be here."

"We're happy to have you," Siren said. "Priest said you're from outside Monterey?"

"Yeah," Xavier said. "I work in marketing out there, but—"

"Hey! What the *fuck!*" Mal barked. He stormed across Ballast, boots heavy on the hardwood and eyes blazing in anger. "What the fuck is *he* doing here?"

"Whoa," I said, one hand on Xavier's shoulder and the other outstretched toward Mal, like I was trying to calm a spooked horse. "What's the problem?"

Mal knocked my hand out of the way and glared daggers at Xavier. "The fucking gall of you to show up here like this," he growled. "The fuck are you doing?"

I hadn't seen Mal look this angry in a long time—probably not since he found out about Bane's involvement in Ankh's death. He clenched his hands into fists at his sides, looking like he was ready to launch himself at Xavier and beat the shit out of him. I glanced around at the other members, but everyone seemed to be just as confused as I was. Even Xavier looked unfazed, smiling placidly in the face of Mal's radiating anger.

But despite the confusion, we trusted Mal, and the other members began to look warily at Xavier.

"I'm here to meet everyone," Xavier said pleasantly. "I'm the new prospect."

"Like fuck you are!" Mal spat back and surged at him.

Luckily, my reflexes were still pretty good, and I caught Mal with a hand on his chest before his fists could connect with Xavier's face. Xavier took a step back, so he was pressed up against the bar, but he still had that same demure smile on his face. Blade and Gunnar both stood at the ready, glancing between Xavier and Mal, and then at each other, as if to try to piece together what was going on and whether they should step in. Blade looked at me, and I could only shrug—I was just as confused as he was.

"Don't act so pissy, baby," Xavier said coolly to Mal. He turned to Blade. "Mal and I are dating. I'm surprised he hasn't mentioned me."

His words ran like ice through my veins. *Dating*? From the way Mal was looking at Xavier, that simply couldn't be true. But there was obviously *something* going on between them. And that weighed unexpectedly heavy on me—the thought of Mal involved with someone else. Especially someone like this.

Why did it, though? It's not like Mal and I were involved—thinking about him with other men *shouldn't* bother me.

And yet this did bother me. *A lot.* Before I could ask any clarifying questions, though, Mal was barreling forward again and brandishing a finger threateningly in Xavier's face.

"We are not *dating*," he said coldly. "We never fucking were, and we never fucking will be. I'm done with your fucking *harassment*—before it was irritating, but now you've crossed the goddamn line."

Harassment? It all began to make sense in my mind. Mal had spent a lot of time recently grimacing at his phone, rejecting calls and deleting texts—had that been Xavier all along? If so, how did all this start? The cold jealousy still weighed heavy in my gut, but now there was confusion, too. How much about Mal's life had I been missing?

"All right," Blade said sternly. He stood between Mal and Xavier, and Gunnar put a firm hand on Xavier's shoulder just in case he tried anything. "Xavier, you better tell us what the fuck is going on here."

Mal crossed his arms over his chest, still looking spitting mad. "First of all, his name's not fucking Xavier."

"That's the name he used when he approached me about prospecting," I said. "And the name we used to run all the background checks. They came out fine."

"It's Stefan," Mal said. "Xavier must be a fake name."

That name sounded slightly familiar. But a fake name didn't make sense—Raven's background checks usually caught a fake name, and this check had come back with full records. So how did...

"Stefan is my middle name," Xavier said with a smirk. "I always use that name when I'm clubbing. Makes things a little more fun, you know?"

"He's fucking stalking me," Mal said. "No way I'm letting his ass prospect with this club, especially after lying through his teeth to Priest. Fuck out of here."

And that was enough explanation for Blade to nod. Gunnar grabbed Xavier by the shoulder roughly and pulled him to the front door—Xavier went, not willingly, but not resisting enough to really get his ass beat.

"This is a fucking disgrace," he shouted over his shoulder. "I thought this club was supposed to be welcoming!"

"Can it," Gunnar said with a growl, and walked him bodily outside. It'd be a few minutes before Gunnar returned— he'd make sure Xavier left the premises, and make sure Xavier knew he wasn't welcome back.

At least not until we figured out what the fuck was going on.

With a sigh, I turned to Mal. He looked suddenly exhausted, sweat beading at his temples as he grimaced and rubbed his forehead.

"All right, Mal," I said with a sigh. "Want to explain what that was all about?"

Chapter 7 - Mal

My heart pounded ferociously in my chest. I was thrumming with energy, and before I realized what I was doing, I started pacing, stalking the width of Ballast near the front door back and forth. Just to try to work off some of the anger burning in my chest.

How dare that little fucker—Stefan, or Xavier, or whatever the fuck his real name was—show up at Ballast? How dare he go behind my back and try to infiltrate my club? And then try to tell everyone we were *dating?* It was such a gross invasion of privacy. I could hardly believe his audacity. Obviously, he was delusional, too, thinking he could show up and I wouldn't kick him out immediately.

He was more obsessed with me than I thought. I sighed and pinched the bridge of my nose as I paced.

"Mal," Blade said. "I need you to explain what's going on here."

I knew I had to, but this was the last place I wanted to do it. In front of the whole club, I'd have to expose some parts of myself I wasn't proud of. I grimaced at the thought— was there a way I could deflect? Put this conversation on pause until it was just Blade and me, in the clubhouse?

I was anxiously thinking of a way to answer Blade when I very nearly walked into Priest. He stood in front of me, hand on my chest, and forcibly stopped my half-conscious pacing.

"Mal," he said in that warm, calming voice of his. "Take a breath."

I did as instructed—a slow, deep breath. My heart stopped pounding so hard. I pressed my lips together, ignoring the concerned gaze of my members around us and focusing instead on the grounding touch of Priest's hand on my chest and his concerned blue eyes.

"Are you in trouble with this guy?" Priest asked. "He's been harassing you?"

"Yeah," I said with a huff. "This is the first time he's actually shown up in person, though."

I expected Priest to share in my frustration, to roll his eyes and call the guy a jackass. What I didn't expect was for Priest to look not concerned or annoyed—but *hurt*.

"Why didn't you say anything?" Priest asked. "How long has this been going on?"

Shit. Priest talked like I'd been actively hiding this from him—and I guessed I had been. I'd thought I could deal with it on my own, and now, Stefan had gone and gotten the rest of the club involved. And from their confused gazes, it was obvious that I wasn't going to be able to get away with talking about this privately. I sighed.

"All right." I raised my voice a little. "I'll explain everything, but I really only want to do it once, so if you want to hear, gather around."

With murmurs of assent, the club members quieted and fixed their attention on me, including the wide-eyed prospects. I hoped this wouldn't drive them away from the club—we needed some fresh blood. Well, if this *did* drive them away, it'd save us some trouble later, I guessed.

"I met Stefan—or Xavier, I guess—last year at Stallions, up in Monterey. I was out there, well…" I cringed a little. No point lying, though. At least Dante and Tru would be glad to be right. "I was out there to get laid. Not looking for anything serious, just blowing off some steam. So I picked him up, brought him to my hotel and that was the end of it."

Priest raised his eyebrows, nodding at me to continue.

"Then a few weeks later, I went back up that way," I said. God, this was embarrassing, laying out the history of my recent hookups to almost every single member of the club. "And Stefan was there again. I usually don't go for repeats, because it complicates things"—I laughed darkly—"as you can see. But at the time it was easy. I didn't have to do the usual song-and-dance of meeting someone. So we hooked up again, and this time exchanged numbers. And I thought maybe I'd have an easy hookup when I needed to blow off some steam, something low pressure, low stakes. Something that didn't matter."

"Seems like it didn't quite go how you expected," Priest said.

"You could say that," I said with a grimace. "He wouldn't stop contacting me for a month. Calling, texting, all that shit. Talking like we were in a relationship, when I'd made it super fucking clear that we were purely casual, and were exchanging numbers for simplicity's sake. And he'd agreed to that! He was—is—delusional. So finally, I answered his calls to tell him to fuck off, and that I didn't want to see him again. Or hear from him, in any capacity."

"And that didn't work either, apparently," Blade said. "You must've really blown his mind."

Stillness fell over the room—and then I laughed. Couldn't help it. Some of the tension in the room broke, and a grin even spread across Priest's concerned face.

"Seems like it," he said. "He really came all the way out here to try to sneak into the club to see you again."

"What'd you do to him?" Tru teased. Then he elbowed Dante. "Must run in the family."

"That guy is *not* Dad's type," Dante said with his eyebrows raised.

"Not what I meant, but thank you for confirming," Tru said delightedly. "So, what is Mal's type, then?"

"Guys," I said warningly, but I couldn't quite keep the smile off my face. It did make my anxiety ease a little, having the usual laughter and teasing floating around the room. Obviously, my boys weren't judging me. "That's not the important thing here."

"Well..." Dante said thoughtfully, then cast his gaze meaningfully at Priest.

"Ah, guys more like *Priest*," Tru said with a serious nod, then pantomimed writing that down on the palm of his hand. "Got it. Let the record state—"

"Tru," Priest said with a big, disbelieving laugh. "That's not the point here."

Then he glanced at me, and his grin softened into something a little closer to a smirk.

Shocked arousal curled hot in my gut. I'd expected Priest to deny Tru a little harder, or just—react a little more seriously. This smirky little acknowledgment was not something I was prepared for. My mouth dropped open, which made Tru cackle.

Then Priest cleared his throat, his expression smoothing into something serious, like he hadn't realized how he was looking at me. "So. This is the first time Stefan's actually shown up face to face with you? Since Stallions?"

"Right," I said. Back to reality. Now was not the time to get distracted by Priest. "It's just been texts and calls, mostly—whenever I block his number, he gets a new one. And he's left some things at the motel. Gifts." I cringed at the memory of coming home to find the packages on the porch, addressed to me with no return address. "Flowers, chocolates... some more suggestive things."

"That's what all those packages were? I thought you were just getting addicted to online shopping," Tru said.

"Well," Star said, "it's clear he's been following you if he knows where you live."

"I know," I admitted, rubbing the back of my neck.

"Why didn't you tell us?" Priest asked.

"I didn't think it was that big of a deal," I admitted. "You saw the guy, he's like a hundred pounds soaking wet. I figured if he showed up, I'd handle it."

"Well, he's obviously escalating things," Rebel said. "I've seen this pattern before. It's textbook stalker behavior."

"I believe this calls for a church meeting tomorrow," Blade said.

Priest nodded and Dante nodded in agreement, and with a sigh, I did too.

"What's the verdict?" Gunnar asked as he shouldered the front door open. "Guy's confirmed off the premises."

"I'll catch you up later," Blade said. "Church tomorrow. For now, though"—he grinned around the room—"let's get back to the fun stuff, shall we?" He swung an arm over Mark's and Paul's shoulders. "So, there's a little taste of how the club works. Never a dull moment…"

As the club members turned back to conversations, drinks, and laughter, I sighed and pressed my fingertips to my temples. This was not how I'd expected my evening to go. And this *was* a serious escalation of Stefan's—Xavier's—behavior. Blade was right—we were going to have to take some sort of action. Irritation and embarrassment roiled in my gut. I hated the thought that I, as co-president, had caused such a ruckus during an event for prospects. Revealing my hookup habits was not a great first impression on them, but hell, I was glad I wouldn't have to explain what had happened over and over, at least.

The way Priest had smirked at me still lingered in my mind. And then—

"Hey," Priest said warmly, as he placed his hand on my shoulder.

I blinked and dropped my hands to my sides again. The rest of the members had resumed the festivities, so it was just Priest and me lingering near the front door. Despite my embarrassment, his presence—as it always did— settled some of my anxieties.

"Hey," I said. "Sorry about all of… that."

Priest shrugged. "Nothing to be sorry for. Xavier's the crazy one." He sighed. "Listen, I don't think you should be riding back to Junee tonight."

"What?" I asked with a start. "You think it's that bad? Gunnar said he was off the premises."

"Yeah," Priest said, "but considering how far he went to get close to you, I wouldn't be surprised if he was lingering somewhere waiting to follow you back. It's not safe."

I wanted to push back, to tell Priest I could handle myself, especially considering that Xavier was just one guy, and we'd have a bunch of us at the Junee clubhouse. I'd caused enough problems tonight, though, all of them leading back to my insistence on handling things on my own. If Priest thought it was best that I stay in Elkin Lake, I was willing to acquiesce to that.

"You can stay at my place," Priest said. "God knows I have the space." He paused. "If that's all right with you."

His hand was still on my shoulder, and he squeezed slightly, sending a small thrill rushing through me, which I quickly shoved aside.

Staying with Priest sounded like a very unique form of torture, but I couldn't deny that the thought of spending more time alone with Priest was appealing, too. Even though nothing would come of it, I always looked forward to having his attention all to myself.

Which was a new sensation for me. Typically, I balked at the idea of staying the night with anyone—especially someone I had some sort of real attraction toward, even if I wasn't going to do anything about that attraction. Spending the night with someone was a kind of intimacy I tried to avoid. And yet, with Priest, it didn't feel as… pressured. It didn't feel like such a risk to the stability I'd so carefully crafted over the years. He cared about my safety, because at the end of the day, we were friends first, and the nature of the club meant we didn't get to spend a whole lot of time focusing on our friendship outside of the rest of our members.

Maybe it'd be good for us both.

"Yeah," I said with a nod. "That sounds good. You're always looking out for us."

"Well, someone's got to," Priest said with a laugh. His gaze darkened and flickered over my face, then down to my chest, then quickly away. "You all are always getting into trouble."

He dropped his hand, and I immediately missed the contact. He turned to lead us out the door, but before he did, I caught his wrist in my hand. Beneath my fingers, his pulse fluttered.

"Hey," I said.

He swallowed. "Yeah?"

His eyes met mine, and suddenly my world narrowed to the smoothness of his skin under my fingertips, and his warm blue eyes.

"Thanks," I murmured.

"Course," Priest said, just as softly, but there was a weight behind it.

Fuck. Whatever that look meant, I wasn't ready to figure out. I dropped my hand and offered a small, albeit awkward smile as I pushed through the front door, trusting Priest would be on my heels. This mess with Xavier was definitely a pain in the ass, and a cause for concern. But the way I felt when Priest looked at me like that—that was the real problem.

Chapter 8 - Priest

Restlessly, I rolled onto my back and stared at the exposed rafters above my bed.

I'd been trying and failing to sleep for hours. Every time I closed my eyes, my brain conjured new images of Mal and that twerp Xavier rolling around in a big Monterey hotel bed. How did Mal fuck him, I wondered? Were they both drunk, fucking sloppily in the dark? Did Mal pin Xavier facedown to the bed and drive relentlessly into him, thighs flexing as he chased his own release? Or maybe Xavier pushed Mal onto his back and rode him, Mal groaning with pleasure as he thrust up into Xavier's tight little body.

Fuck. I pushed the heels of my hands into my eyes. And Mal had been lying to us for months about this guy—not letting any of us know about the extent of his harassment. Maybe Xavier didn't *look* like a threat, but how he looked didn't mean anything. I remembered Dylan, who'd looked like the most average, clean-cut guy I could imagine and had nearly killed Jonah trying to get him back from Maverick. Mal keeping something like this from the club wasn't just a danger to his own safety—it was a danger to the entire club. Mal knew better than that. So why had he been so intent on keeping this a secret?

Did he have other secrets I didn't know about?

I knew I wasn't privy to all the details of Mal's life, but it was jarring to have something like this, something so big, revealed so suddenly. Especially because he wasn't just my president—he was one of my closest friends.

Sleep was obviously a lost cause at this point. No use pretending anymore. I sat up in bed and sighed. I figured I'd sneak into the kitchen for a cup of tea or a nightcap, something to help me catch a few hours before the sun came up.

I stood and pulled on a pair of sweatpants; I figured Mal wouldn't appreciate me wandering me into the kitchen the way I usually slept, naked. Or—the way he'd looked at me in Ballast leaped to the front of my mind. When Tru had made some crack about me being his type, I couldn't help but smirk at the remark, expecting Mal to howl his disagreement. But instead, he'd just looked at me, his mouth slightly open, eyes wide and gleaming with interest.

So maybe he *would* appreciate it.

I shook my head. That didn't matter—he was here for his own protection, not because I was horny. I'd offered my place instead of the clubhouse because, as I'd said, I *did* have the space, and we were both too old to listen to the members fuck through the walls. Not to turn things into a booty call, or whatever the kids called it these days.

I descended the stairs carefully, assuming Mal would be knocked out on the couch, hopefully sleeping better than I was. To my surprise, though, one of the lamps was turned on, casting the room in dim yellow light. Mal was sitting up on the couch, with the framed photo of Ankh from the hearth in his hands. He was lost in thought, so fixated on the photo that he didn't notice me at all. Not until I turned the sink on to fill the kettle with hot water.

Mal started, nearly dropping the photo—he fumbled it a little, then set it on the coffee table with a grimace. "You scared me."

"Sorry," I said with a grin. "I do that a lot."

Mal peered over his shoulder curiously at me. "Scare people?"

"No," I chuckled as I flipped on the electric kettle. "Look at that picture. Ask Ankh for advice."

With a heavy sigh, Mal leaned back against the couch. "I could use some of his advice right now."

I fixed two mugs of tea, then walked to the couch and sat down beside Priest. "Can't sleep?"

"Just a lot on my mind," Mal said. He nodded gratefully for the tea, then wrapped his hands around the mug, with his gaze still on the picture on the coffee table. "What about you?"

Not like I could tell him I was tossing and turning fantasizing about him plowing Xavier. "About the same," I said. "I'm no Ankh, but... what's on your mind?"

Gazing into the depths of his mug, Mal suddenly looked exhausted. I wondered if I should've left him alone—if I was crossing some unknown boundary asking him to open up to me like this, in the dim, intimate light of my cabin. And yet, my hesitation wasn't enough for me to withdraw my question. Not when Mal looked so tense. Tense and lost. He needed someone to talk to.

"I just... I'm not looking forward to this church meeting tomorrow," Mal admitted with a grimace. "I just don't think Xavier is *that* big of a threat. Certainly not big enough to warrant an emergency church meeting."

I set my mug down. Whatever I was expecting Mal to admit was bothering him, it wasn't this.

"Clearly, he's a little unbalanced," Mal admitted. "But he's just one guy. This didn't need to get escalated into a problem for the entire club. At the end of the day, it's my personal business, and—and I can handle it. I *should* be the one to handle it, not the rest of the club."

"Well," I said, tamping down on the frustration flaring in my chest, "the rest of the club got involved when Xavier lied about wanting to prospect to get close to you."

Mal exhaled, visibly frustrated. He tightened his grip on the mug. "Yeah, I can admit that was fucked up. But it's still—"

"Come on, Mal," I interrupted. "You *know* it's club business. You know better than this."

Mal said nothing, and the frustration inside me burned a little hotter. Sometimes I felt like I was the only person in this club with any sense. I understood that it was embarrassing, but the safety of the club was more important than Mal's pride. And I *knew* somewhere in his head, he knew that. He just had blinders on—he'd decided that Xavier wasn't dangerous and was ignoring the blatant warning signs so he didn't have to reveal his hookup to the club. Not that it was anything to be embarrassed about.

"Our club has been through so much shit," I said. "We've seen how things work out when we ignore situations like this or try to handle them on our own. Don't you remember Dylan? Or Jono?"

"Of course I do," Mal said. "This isn't the same."

"Maybe it's not the same," I said, "but it's in that same realm. You're the co-president, Mal, you can't afford to look the other way on situations like this. And it's not just personal anymore. You need to be an example of how to handle things maturely and responsibly, with the support of the club."

"I see what you're saying," Mal said. "Does this really warrant a church meeting, though? We've blacklisted Xavier—what else is there to do?"

Again, my frustration flared. It seemed insane to me that Mal didn't see why this was such a big deal. He'd been lying to the club—hiding months of harassment from a guy that knew where he *lived*. Which also happened to be club property. What if Xavier hadn't tried to prospect? What if he'd done something worse, like break into the house, or follow Mal until he got him alone? We were *lucky* it'd gone as harmlessly as it had.

"I've had more than enough of seeing my loved ones put unnecessarily in harm's way," I said a little sharply. "He knows where you live! He could be out there tonight, waiting for you to come home so he can—I don't know, break in and do something fucked up now that you've publicly rejected him." The thought made my skin crawl, and I pushed my hands through my hair despairingly. "I don't want to lose one of my oldest friends to some psycho he fucked. Especially to some scrawny twink. Seriously, you can do better."

Mal raised his eyebrows. "You think so?"

I looked up, and Mal was biting back a little smile.

Okay. So maybe that outburst wasn't totally warranted. Maybe *I* was acting a little crazy. "Sorry," I muttered. "Just a little stressed out."

"Yeah, I can tell," Mal said with a warm, but hesitant chuckle. "Maybe we both could use some of Ankh's advice these days."

I laughed a little, too, leaning back into the couch and taking a sip of my tea.

"You're right, though," Mal said. "I just… I just didn't want the club *this* involved in my personal life. I'm not exactly proud of my hookups. And recognizing that there *is* danger means involving everyone else in the aftereffects of *my* bad decisions." He sighed. "I'm the president. I should've known better than to get involved with a guy like that."

"How would you have known?" I asked gently. "Not like he was wearing a sign that said, 'I'm deranged.'"

"That certainly would've made things easier," Mal grumbled.

"And yeah," I acknowledged, "you're the co-president. Which is why we're going to handle this as a club. And not wait for him to show up again and escalate his harassment even more."

Mal nodded, then set his tea down. "Thanks." He pressed his lips together, then his hand fell to my thigh, just above my knee. It was a gentle, reassuring touch, and when I met his gaze, his eyes were soft and thoughtful. His hand resting on my thigh sent sparks careening across my skin, jolting me even more awake. "You always know how to talk some sense into me."

"I've had a lot of practice," I murmured.

It felt good being this close to Mal—warm and enticing in the low light of the room. It was one of those rare moments when all my responsibilities seemed to fall away, something that hadn't happened in far too long. I was used to being the one who had to be strong and decisive— as vice president, and a senior member, I was the pillar the members leaned on for support. But with Mal, it didn't feel that way. We held *each other* up, with a natural ease I hadn't felt with anyone since... Since Ankh.

I knew I didn't have to worry about Mal's capacity to handle this situation. I could trust him to make the right decision regarding Xavier. With that knowledge, suddenly this conversation wasn't about the club.

It was about us.

I felt drawn toward Mal. I wanted him, in a way I hadn't wanted anyone but Ankh in years. And I knew Mal felt it too. He moved his hand, his palm sliding over the fabric of my sweatpants, his fingers barely pressing into the muscle of my thigh.

He leaned closer.

This was happening.

And I was leaning closer, too, as if I were being pulled toward him like a puppet on a string.

He wanted me.

And I wanted him, just as badly. Wanted to feel his full lips against mine, his callused hand on my cheek; I wanted him to press me into the couch and cover me with his strong body and forget about Xavier.

Forget.

My blood ran ice-cold in my veins, and I jerked backward, breaking the hypnotic spell between us. What the fuck was I thinking?

"Sorry," I said a little lamely. "I'm, uh—" I stood up and stubbed my toe on the coffee table in my haste. "Shit!"

"Are you all right?" Mal asked tentatively.

"Yeah," I said, but I really wasn't. I'd almost *kissed* him. "Sorry. Get some sleep. Holler if you need anything."

Before Mal could answer, and before he could see the flush coloring my cheeks, I turned and hurried back up the stairs to my bedroom.

In my room, I promptly sat at the foot of the bed and buried my face in my hands.

I'd wanted Mal to forget about Xavier by kissing me. But was I doing the same thing? Trying to forget about Ankh? Logically, I knew it wasn't the same thing—not even close—but I couldn't ignore the swirl of guilt roiling in my gut. I'd come so close to making such a foolish mistake. I couldn't just impulsively kiss my oldest friend—and he wasn't just *my* friend, he was a friend of Ankh's, too. In fact, I'd never known Mal without Ankh by my side, not until Ankh's passing.

And regardless of how I'd felt in the living room, this wasn't just about us. We had the club to worry about. We had to deal with Xavier—there was enough confusion surrounding the club right now, and enough danger in the air. I didn't need to complicate this situation further. And what if things went south between us? Was I ready to drag the club into that mess, too? Because a relationship between us two would affect the whole club. Not to mention a not-so-small part of me worried what the club might think. Even if I was ready to open my heart to Mal, would the club be ready to see me with someone who wasn't Ankh?

Would my son be ready?

There were too many factors to consider when it came to me and Mal, and it wasn't fair to put that on everyone else.

No matter how badly I wanted him.

Chapter 9 - Mal

Somehow, against all odds, I'd gotten a little bit of sleep on Priest's deep, comfortable couch. I'd drifted off as dawn was threatening to break, and when I'd woken up, Priest wasn't there. He'd left a note, though, letting me know he'd see me later at the clubhouse for church.

So I'd gone back to the motel to clean up and get a change of clothes, then headed straight back into Elkin Lake for the mid-morning meeting. I was on my third or fourth coffee, leaning against the counter as the usual morning chaos unfolded around me. The leadership and the enforcement team were all here, drinking coffee and fighting over leftover pastries from Stella's.

But Priest wasn't here yet, and I cringed at the thought that he might be avoiding me.

Obviously, Priest hadn't wanted to stick around this morning and talk about the almost-kiss. I wasn't too keen on talking about it, either, though the reasonable part of me knew that we *should.*

There was something between us—that much was clear. He felt as strongly as I did, at least in terms of attraction. I'd seen that in the way he'd leaned toward my touch on the couch, like we'd both gotten caught up in the wave of attraction between us, and nearly been dragged out to sea. I'd been willing to kiss him, too. I'd really thought it was going to happen—and I couldn't deny that I'd felt a bolt of disappointment when he'd pulled away, unwilling to act on the desire between us.

Why had I been so disappointed? I'd already decided not to act on the way I felt for him. But now that I knew he felt it, too… something had shifted inside me.

In the kitchen, Dante pulled Heath into a brief kiss before he smiled and murmured something into Heath's ear that made him blush. I was beyond thrilled that my son had found someone who matched him so well, and his concern for my own lack of love life had made me wonder about my future in a way I hadn't in a long time.

I'd put aside any thoughts of finding a partner after Melanie left, at first consciously and then just out of habit. It just didn't seem worth the trouble. I wasn't hooking up often, but it was enough to keep me from going crazy from sexual frustration. Now, though, the pleasure I got from random hookups didn't seem worth it, either—especially since the last hookup had landed me a fucking stalker.

Looking around the clubhouse at all the members gathered to address this situation that I had caused, I felt fairly certain I wouldn't be hooking up at Stallions ever again.

Was it really such a big deal that Priest and I were friends first? If we both felt the attraction between us, why *not* act on it? We were both adults. And we were both experienced enough to know that acting on attraction didn't mean we were committing to anything more than that. It didn't have to be anything serious if that wasn't what we wanted. Maybe it was something we both needed—a way to blow off steam safely.

Wasn't sure how I was going to convince Priest of that, though. Or even how to breach the topic. Maybe it was better if we just pretended last night didn't happen.

"All right, guys," Blade said, his booming voice carrying easily over the chatter of the room. "Let's get started." I grabbed my coffee and took my seat at the table.

As if on cue, the front door swung open, and Priest walked in with his cheeks reddened from the chilly wind outside. He approached me with a broad grin and sat down next to me, touching my shoulder in greeting, and some of the anxiety I felt was relieved. Honestly, I was surprised, too. I'd expected things to be awkward, at least a little, since he'd purposefully avoided me that morning. If Priest had acted like he was uncomfortable, or continued to avoid me, that would've hurt worse than his rejection last night did. Maybe he'd just needed some space, take a few breaths, figure out what was happening. That much I could understand.

The room settled down, with members of the inner circle and the enforcement team gathered around the table.

"Let's cut straight to the chase," Blade said. "I know none of us are happy that Xavier slipped through the cracks like that. So let's figure out how to seal them—and what to do about this stalker."

"Right," Raven said. He wrinkled his nose at his laptop, obviously frustrated that his background check hadn't caught Xavier earlier. "I'll dig deeper into his background to start—see if he has a history of this kind of stuff."

"I've been talking to some guys at the station," Rebel added with a nod. "You've definitely got a cause for a restraining order here."

"A restraining order?" I asked, raising both my eyebrows in surprise. "You really think that's necessary?"

A restraining order was something for people who were in real danger—threats and stalking and all that.

Which.

I supposed Xavier *had* been doing those things. But it felt excessive for someone like me, who could easily whoop Xavier's ass if I needed to, even without the entire club behind me. A restraining order felt like something meant for people who couldn't protect themselves.

"Yeah," Rebel said. "I really do. If you put it in place now, if he pulls something again, legally we'll have a stronger case. Easier to get him put away."

I opened my mouth to push back again and was rewarded with Priest's elbow knocking into mine. He narrowed his eyes at me, mouth quirked into a little smile, and he didn't need words to say exactly what he meant. I was being bullheaded again—letting my pride get in the way of the safety of the club. Because Rebel was right. It was better to stay ahead of Xavier, rather than wait for him to do something even crazier.

"All right," I relented. "As long as the process isn't too big of a pain in the ass."

"Oh, it definitely is," Rebel said with a laugh. "But I'll walk you through it at the station."

"And until we figure out where he is and what his plans are, we want you to have a regular watch," Blade said. "Gunnar, Tru, and the enforcement team have already put together a schedule to ensure you've got someone on your six twenty-four seven."

"What? Full watch? Guys." I glanced around the table, and all the enforcers, from both chapters, were nodding. "*Seriously*?"

"Seriously," Gunnar said. "He knows where you *live*, Mal."

"You'd do the same thing for us," Siren said, leaning back in her chair. "If any of us were dealing with this kind of stalking, you'd be calling for these same measures— maybe even more."

I pressed my lips together.

Siren raised both eyebrows, peering down her nose at me as she waited for me to argue otherwise. But how could I? She was right. If any of the members had someone sending them messages for months, sending things to their home, and then showing up at the bar as a prospect—hell, I'd've called the cavalry ages ago.

"You've been looking after the club for years," Tru said. "Let us do the same for you, for once."

I sighed. "Okay, okay. But only until we get the restraining order set up."

"I think the sergeants get to decide when the watch ends," Blade said with a grin. "Nice try, though."

Raven pulled up the enforcement schedule, and the rest of the meeting was spent hashing out the enforcement rotation, as well as plans of action for if Xavier did show up or sent more mail. Raven did something complicated to my phone, too, pulling records of all the numbers that Xavier had used, and he grimaced at the sheer amount of them.

I really hadn't thought it was this serious. But the club's reaction was making it obvious that I'd been in denial about how serious this was. I hadn't heard from Xavier since he was kicked out of Ballast, but I knew it wouldn't be long before I did again. If I knew anything about him, it was that he was relentless.

The meeting adjourned. I was heading back to Junee, but not without two enforcers at my back—luckily it was Eli and Star to start, since they were heading back to Junee anyway. I hated that I was causing so much trouble, but they were right. If one of my members got themselves a stalker, I wouldn't blame *them*. And yet I couldn't help blaming myself. This wasn't my first rodeo; I should've known better about Xavier.

With a sigh, I headed out to my bike, and I didn't have to look to know that Eli and Star were heading toward their bikes, as well. Just before I pulled on my helmet, though, a familiar voice called, "Mal, wait a second."

I turned around, and Priest was striding down the stairs, looking determined. Surprised, I tilted my head. "What's up?"

"I just…" Priest paused, standing close, but not *too* close. He rubbed the back of his neck. "I wanted to apologize for last night."

Well, that wasn't what I was expecting. I blinked. "Apologize?"

"Yeah," Priest admitted. "I acted like a moron. I was just— surprised."

"I was too," I said. Were we really talking about this? After Priest had left that morning, I was sure we'd just pretend it never happened.

"I didn't know how to handle that kind of moment," Priest said, his face flushed slightly. "I still don't. Obviously, there's something there but—I don't know what we should do. Or if we should do anything."

His blue eyes flicked up to mine, and my breath caught in my chest. Feeling the attraction between us in the depths of evening, in private, was one thing, but hearing him acknowledge it aloud like this sent a new wave of desire through me—of *hope*. Priest looked so open and earnest when he said it, too, and I was gripped by the sudden urge to pull him in and kiss that insecure look off his face.

But if he didn't want that last night, he certainly didn't want it now. Still, just acknowledging the spark between us felt grounding. Comforting.

"I don't know what we should do either," I said. "But I don't think we *need* to do anything. I'm—I'm okay with things as they are."

Priest's face softened into something like relief, the furrow smoothing from his brow as his lips curved into a smile. "Good," he said. "I just wanted to make sure things were okay between us."

"Of course they are," I said. "And I'm sorry again about all of this. This mess with Xavier."

"Nothing to be sorry for," Priest said. He placed a hand on my shoulder and squeezed firmly. Even in the light of day, instead of in the privacy of his cabin, his touch still sent new sparks across my skin. "Just take care of yourself, okay? And call me if you need anything."

"Thanks," I said. "Really."

"Ready to roll out, boss!" Eli said pointedly.

I looked up to see more than a handful of members on the porch watching us, including Dante and Tru. I cringed at Priest, and he matched my expression before breaking into a laugh. Yeah, I'd likely get grilled about this later—and Priest would, too. But whatever wringer the guys were going to put me through, it was worth knowing that things were okay between us. For now, at least.

Chapter 10 - Priest

I stared up into the engine above me. It definitely needed new gaskets, and the oil pan seals could use replacement, too. Relatively minor work, but the kind of repairs I liked doing. Keeping my hands busy was good for my head, good for my grief. I liked helping out at Ankhor Works as often as I could, since it was the business I could actually help out the most—I knew if I tried to step foot into the kitchen at Stella's, Dante would chase me out brandishing a spatula like a weapon.

Ankhor Works had a special place in my heart, too. Ballast was the first place Ankh and I opened together, but Ankhor Works was the first business that a member had brought to the club. When Maverick had asked about turning his family business into a club business, I'd almost been too shocked to speak. It was exactly what we'd wanted the club to be—family. Ankhor Works had thrived as a club business, and it was a place for me to connect with the members. I'd had a hell of a lot of good conversations with the members while we were poking around in engines. Something about working together invited good conversation.

After Ankh passed, I spent more time at the garage. It was the first place I started going again, once I'd been able to crawl out of bed instead of being frozen and exhausted with grief. Working here had helped me heal, and seeing my brothers thrive was a big part of that.

Even from under this beat-up old sedan, I could hear Maverick's laugh, and Grace's squeal of delight.

We'd been through a hell of a lot as a club. I couldn't be prouder of my members.

I rolled out from under the car to grab the correct sized wrench. And as I started working at loosening an old rusted-in nut, I couldn't help but acknowledge the slight ache in my chest.

I'd finally felt like I was healing, and now, whatever was happening between Mal and me was throwing a wrench (so to speak) into that. I'd expected my life from now on would be simple, quiet—devoted to the club. I didn't think I'd ever be interested in anyone again. Not in a way where I actually wanted to do something about it.

And yet whenever I saw Mal, my heart pounded, and desire and nerves swirled in my chest. It made me feel young again, on the precipice of something new, and the chance to feel that way again was more than I ever expected.

Since Ankh was the only man I'd been with, the desire was strange, and intoxicating, and sometimes confusing. It was intimidating. It made me feel a little guilty. And I never thought my desire for Mal would ever progress beyond that—a feeling.

I hadn't expected Mal to acknowledge that he wanted me, too.

Mal had been busy the past few days, first with Rebel getting the restraining order in place, and then trying to figure out the routine of his daily life now that he had enforcers on his tail twenty-four seven. So far we hadn't heard anything from Xavier—which was a relief. But at the same time, it made me a little nervous. I had a feeling it wasn't going to be the last that we heard of him, and every day that passed in silence made me more anxious about what was to come. I hated the thought of Xavier hiding out somewhere, biding his time, figuring out how to best get to Mal.

This rusted old nut wasn't budging an inch, and I was starting to feel it in my hands and my wrists. I couldn't spend hours and hours under an engine anymore, like I could when I was a younger man. With a sigh, I slid out from under the car, intending to find a chemical remover to work at the gaskets, and take a break to stretch out my wrists.

I clambered off the ratty old creeper and got to my feet. I grabbed a rag, then rubbed at the sweat gathering on the back of my neck. A prickle ran down my spine—I was being watched. I moved slowly. Maybe if I pretended I didn't notice it anyone was there, they'd leave me alone. Because I had a sense of what this was going to be about.

Behind me, someone cleared their throat.

I turned around. Waiting with eyebrows raised was Raven, with Logan and Jonah on either side of them.

"Oh, boy," I said automatically. I knew that look on my son's face, and I was about to get grilled.

"Hey, Pop," Raven said with a grin. "Need a break?"

"I think I'm taking one whether I want to or not," I said with a laugh.

Raven nodded, then grinned at Logan and Jonah and guided me out the garage back door into the gravel lot behind the building. Outside, a bunch of the guys were lingering: Rebel and Jazz were sitting in the bed of one of the club trucks, beers in hand, while Dawson and Heath leaned against the side. Brennan and Beau were there, too, in their work clothes leaning against Brennan's truck. I closed the door to Ankhor Works behind me, feeling suddenly like I'd walked into the lion's den.

"So," I said, glancing around at all my brothers-in-arms. "What's this about?"

"Don't look so nervous," Logan said with a laugh. "We just wanted to stop by and say hello."

I raised my eyebrows. "Now I know that's a crock of shit."

"What?" Jonah asked. "We can't stop by and say hello to our vice?"

"Sure, you can," I said. "Don't look so innocent. Come on, guys, cut to the chase. I've got work to finish up."

Jonah laughed, then nodded, admitting it. "All right, so maybe there was an ulterior motive."

"We're just curious," Jazz said, leaning forward with a predatory smile on his face. "There's obviously something going on between you and Mal."

"Jazz," Raven said with exasperation. "We were supposed to ease into it."

"What? Come on, we all *know.*" Jazz grinned at me. "We're here to help."

"You sure about that?" I raised my eyebrows.

"He wouldn't shut up about you," Rebel said with a shrug. "Mal, I mean. At the station. It was cute—made him embarrassed. Like he kept catching himself talking about you without meaning to."

My heart pounded. I felt like a kid, gossiping with my friends at lunch about who liked who. There was a sweet kind of thrill to it—I never thought I'd feel this young and giddy again. And yet the thought of Mal talking Rebel's ear off about me did exactly that. I grinned at my feet, and the guys whistled and knocked their elbows into each other's sides.

"All right, all right," I said. "I'm only talking because I'm so outnumbered here."

"We're all on the same team," Brennan said.

"Yeah, *your* team!" Heath agreed.

"So maybe there's something different about our relationship these days," I admitted.

"Meaning…" Jonah prompted.

"You guys are relentless," I said fondly. "Yeah, okay, I'm—I'm attracted to him."

The guys started hooting and hollering, of course, but they calmed down when I held my hand up to indicate I wasn't done speaking. "I'm not blind, of course, I've always thought he was handsome. But until recently I'd never felt…"

"Into it?" Beau offered.

"Right," I said. "But that doesn't mean anything is going to happen."

"Sure," Logan said, sounding exceedingly unconvinced of that.

"I'm serious," I said. "Just because I feel it doesn't mean we should act on it. I don't know if I'm ready for that."

The excitement cooled off a little, and the guys nodded. "Well," Jazz said, "If you ever decide you *are*, I can give some tips on things Mal likes. You know, restaurants, candle fragrances… things like that."

Brennan grinned and nodded. "Me too, you know. He helped a lot with the cabin design, so I have a sense of his taste…"

"Same," Logan said. "I'm great at wooing."

"I don't know if that's true," Jonah said thoughtfully. "When's the last time you went on a date?"

"None of your business," Logan said primly.

"Guys, guys," I said through a laugh. "Good to know I've got wingmen if I need it."

"Or *when*," Beau corrected.

After some more teasing and hoots, most of the guys went on their way—Brennan and Beau back to work, some of the members back to the clubhouse, and Jonah and Heath back into Ankhor Works to rescue Maverick where he was manning the lobby with Grace and Gretel.

Then it was just Raven and me, leaning against the back wall of the shop in the cool air. With the members gone, it was suddenly a lot quieter, and Raven's teasingly knowing expression melted into something a little more curious.

"You arranged all this, didn't you?" I asked.

"Maybe," Raven said with a shrug. "Just thought you could use some outside opinions."

I paused, nodding as I turned that thought over. It was kind of Raven to wrangle all the guys together like this, but I couldn't shake the instinct that the feelings I had for Mal were a small kind of betrayal to our family. Even if logically I knew that wasn't the case, it still *felt* like that.

"How do you feel about it?" I asked him. "Me and Mal. Really."

"Really?" Raven asked.

My heart sank a little—I couldn't stand the thought of Raven going along with this because he felt like he *should*. When maybe, really, he wasn't ready to move on, either. His happiness was the most important thing in the world to me.

"Pop," Raven said with his hand on my forearm. "I'm happy for you. *Beyond* happy."

I blinked, surprised. "I—you're okay with it?"

"Yeah," he said with a laugh. "Of course I am. I know it's been hard, but—but I think you deserve to find someone, you know? I want you to be happy. Dad would want you to be happy."

I folded my hand over his and swallowed around the sudden knot in my throat. Raven had grown into such a strong and generous young man—I could hardly believe this was the same bratty kid Ankh and I had raised together. I'd always been able to tell when he was lying; he never could hide it well. And from the soft look in his deep blue eyes—a look that mirrored Ankh's eyes almost exactly—I knew he was being honest.

"I am happy," I said.

"I know you are," Raven said. "And you know that's not what I mean."

I sighed. "It's that obvious?"

"That you're lonely? Yeah, it is." Raven smiled and shook his head a little. "I was a little worried about you getting back in the dating game, honestly—I know that process isn't easy. But Mal… I mean, it's *Mal.* He's a good guy. And Ankh loved him, too, you know."

"You don't think it's too soon?" I cringed as soon as I asked, then pressed my lips together. "It hasn't been that long. I feel guilty, you know, like I shouldn't feel anything for anyone. Even if is Mal."

"It's been over two years, Pop," Raven said. "Just because you feel something for Mal doesn't mean you didn't love Dad."

My heart clenched at his words, and suddenly the knot in my throat was too big to speak around.

"Dad wouldn't want you to beat yourself up for feeling something like this for someone else," Raven said. "It only means you've got a big heart. And a lot of love to give."

"Jesus, kid," I said, a little choked, and then pulled Raven into a rough hug. "When'd you get so smart?"

Raven huffed a laugh into my shoulder, returning the hug and squeezing me hard. "No idea. Definitely not from the guys that raised me."

Hearing Raven put it in such a way made some of the anxiety inside me ease. Ankh wouldn't want me to suffer. And we'd both loved Mal, trusted him as our closest friend. If there was anyone that Ankh would be happy to see me end up with, it'd be Mal.

"Thanks," I said.

"Life's short," Raven said as he pulled away. "I don't think Dad would want you to let this pass you by."

"Maybe you're onto something." I felt a little more at ease—knowing I had Raven's blessing lifted a weight I hadn't realized I was carrying. And yet I still wasn't completely sure if this was the right decision. I didn't need to figure it all out right this second, though. I could take the first step and see where it brought me. "Maybe I'll talk to Mal."

Raven's expression brightened. "Really?"

"Yeah," I said with a small smile. "I don't know if this will go anywhere—or even if it should—but I should at least talk to him, right?"

"Hell, yeah, you should," Raven said. He pulled me into another hug. "I think this could be really good for both of you, Pop."

"But no pressure," I said with a short laugh.

"Right," Raven said, leaning back and flashing a toothy grin. "No pressure."

Chapter 11 - Mal

"So," I said, smoothing my hand over the map of Elkin Lake I had spread out on the table at Stella's. "That's a rundown of the club borders, and a quick explanation of who patrols what areas, depending on chapters. Any questions so far?"

Mark and Paul looked admittedly a little dumbfounded— likely they weren't expecting to get a geography crash- course as part of their prospecting. And they probably weren't expecting to do it in a bakery, either. Stella's was the best place to meet mid-morning, though, with virtually unlimited coffee and a chance for me to show Mark and Paul around one of the club's prized businesses.

"Thanks, Mal," Blade said, from where he was seated at my side. "So now let me go over some of our major businesses, starting with Ankhor Works."

Mark and Paul both nodded in unison, heads bobbing like a pair of chickens. At least they were eager.

I sighed and glanced toward the big glass window at the front of Stella's. Outside, Siren and Coop were leaning against their bikes, chatting as they each sipped at a cup of to-go coffee. As co-president, I was used to having enforcers at my back, especially when things had gotten dicey in the past with the now-defunct Vipers or the sometimes-tetchy Empire.

But knowing that Siren and Coop were here because of a single irritating kid and my own bad decision... it itched at me. Even though I'd agreed to it, and I knew that the club members were right, it still felt like a waste of our resources. We hadn't heard a peep from Xavier since he'd been kicked out of Ballast—did I really need to have *two* enforcers watching me at all times? Especially when I was on club premises?

Blade finished running through the businesses, and then instructed Mark and Paul to stand up.

"We all pitch in at all the businesses," Blade said, "so I figured Dante could give you a quick tour of the Stella's kitchen before we move on."

Dante strolled out of the kitchen, wiping his hands on his apron, and waved the prospects behind the counter. That left me and Blade alone at the table, and I was grateful for the break.

Blade sighed and stretched his arms overhead, then took a long sip of his coffee. "Seems like these kids will do fine."

"Yeah, I think so," I agreed.

The rest of the day was to be spent showing the prospects around the other businesses—Ballast and Ankhor Works, primarily, and then having them spend a relaxed evening at the clubhouse with the rest of the members. Just to see how they fit in. It was going to be busy, and while I was looking forward to it, I still felt a little restless. It'd been a few days since I'd seen Priest, not since we'd acknowledged our mutual desire outside of the clubhouse... and then decided to keep it under wraps. Now that I had a moment with Blade, I couldn't keep the lid on my curiosity.

"So," I said. "How's—how's Priest been?"

Blade wrinkled his nose, then shrugged a little. "He's fine, I guess."

"You guess?" I asked.

"Well, you know," Blade said. "As far as I can tell, things may have changed."

He glanced meaningfully at me, then took another sip of his coffee.

Back in the kitchen, the prospects were intensely focused on whatever Dante was explaining—potentially the difference between the proofing box and the walk-in?—so it was clear we'd have a few minutes to ourselves. So I sighed and nodded.

"You'd be right about that," I said.

Blade nodded. He was clearly itching to say more but pressed his lips together like he was holding back. Under the table, I nudged his foot with mine.

"Just say what you want to say," I said warmly. "Prez to prez." If anyone deserved to have an opinion on whatever was developing between Priest and me, it was Blade.

Blade sighed and wrapped both hands around his mug of coffee, then turned a little in his seat so he was facing me. "You know I want both of you to be happy," he said.

"There's a but coming, isn't there?" I said with a smile, hiding the twist of nerves in my chest. If Blade didn't think that Priest and I exploring this was okay, I'd have to seriously reconsider. He was my co-president, after all, and if we weren't on the same page, the leadership structure of the whole club was in danger.

"Not a 'but'," Blade said. "I'm invested in both of you being *happy*—I'm not necessarily invested in things working out one way or another. But I want to make sure that we two are communicating about what a change in your relationship would mean for the club."

Some of my nerves settled. That was a valid concern, and one that I should've brought up with Blade earlier, when I realized this wasn't going to go away as easily as I'd hoped. I'd been so caught up in my own feelings, and how to navigate the changing waters with Priest, that I'd left my presidential duties on the back burner. That was the benefit of having a co-president: we helped each other pick up the slack.

"You know," I said, "this is why Ankh chose you to be president. You've got it, Blade, right down to your core."

Blade grinned. "Stop trying to distract me."

"I'm not!" I said with a laugh. "I'm being honest. We should've talked about this earlier."

"I trust both of you," Blade said. "But—I have to make sure that *you* know that the club comes first."

"I do know," I said. "And Priest does, too. I think that's part of the reason my feelings are changing, you know? I haven't been interested in anyone in so long in this way, but with Priest… I know our priorities are the same. I know I can trust him. At this point in my life, I can't imagine being with anyone who isn't as connected to the club as I am."

"He's family," Blade said, nodding with understanding.

"Right," I said. "This feels more like… a progression, rather than something new. If that makes sense."

"It does," Blade said. "Really."

"But I want to make sure it's okay with you, too," I said. "Not just as co-president, but as a member. My relationship with Priest has always been different than yours."

Priest had always been a friend to me—one of my best. But he'd been closer to a father figure to Blade, from Blade's early years with the club and later as he'd developed as president. Blade had leaned heavily on Priest for guidance and support, and I didn't want Blade to think I was trying to pull Priest away from his duties as vice.

"Honestly?" Blade asked.

"Honestly."

"I think it'd be good for the club," Blade said. "Merging the clubs has been good, but there's still some distance between the chapters, you know? I think it'd make us feel more like a family."

"Using us to unite the chapters?" I teased. "Always with the presidential thinking."

Blade rolled his eyes. "Come on. You know I'm right."

I peered at him curiously. "You're not worried about what might happen to the club if it *doesn't* work out?"

Even asking that ached—there wasn't even anything *between* Priest and me, besides the mutually acknowledged attraction. Not yet. And the attraction didn't mean anything would happen. But part of being presidents meant we had to think about all the potential ways it could shake out. Even if I wasn't sure how I *wanted* it to shake out. Because regardless of the attraction between us, this was *Priest*. A small, weak part of me couldn't help but think there was no way I could live up to Ankh's memory. Whatever we had, if we had anything at all, wouldn't compare to what Priest had with Ankh.

But I owed it to him to at least talk it through.

"Of course, I am," Blade said. "But it's like you said. The club's family to you both. It might be rocky, but we'd work it out."

"You sound pretty sure of that," I said.

"I am," Blade said with a nod. "But more than that—both you and Priest have lost a lot. And given more than anyone else to our club. And you both deserve a real shot at happiness, even if there are risks." He grinned. "Come on, we're Hell's Ankhor. You can't say we don't get off on a little risk."

"You got me there," I said.

"Just talk to him," Blade said. "Sounds to me like you've both got your priorities straight. Now you just need to figure out the next steps together."

He made it sound so easy. And admittedly it felt a little easier, knowing that Blade wasn't horrified that there was something growing between Priest and me—and having the confidence that even if shit did hit the fan between us, the club would be able to weather it. It was like Blade said: we'd both given so much, and lost so much, too. We'd figure out a way through whatever comes next.

"All right," I said. "I will."

"Good," Blade said, clapping me on the back with a grin.

Dante strolled back out with the prospects in tow, who both looked equal parts excited and terrified.

"I think they got the gist of it," Dante said with a grin. "Would love to get them in here for a few shifts next week, see if either of them have a knack for baking."

"Thanks, Dante," Blade said. "I bet we can make that happen. But for now, come on, guys, let's stop by the motel and grab a bite before we head into Elkin Lake to Ballast."

I nodded in agreement, and the four of us filed outside to meet Siren and Coop, leaving Dante to man the bakery. In the middle of the day, the motel was likely to be empty, with all the guys either at work or on shifts for the club, especially with a big night planned later. And admittedly, when members weren't busy, they ended up more often at the Elkin Lake clubhouse nowadays—the new renovation was still novel.

We rode the short distance from Stella's to the motel.

"It's leftovers for lunch, guys," Blade said as he unlocked the front door and then waved the prospects in. "But they're good leftovers, I'm telling you, Star is getting really into smoking meats…"

I lingered on the porch with my phone in hand. Blade was right—I needed to talk to Priest. Sooner rather than later, before I could chicken out. And just as I was about to call him to see if he wanted to grab a coffee, a familiar rumble cut through the quiet of the afternoon.

Priest parked his bike right next to mine. He climbed off, pulled off his helmet, and shot me a wide grin that made my stomach flip. I noticed every shift of muscle in his shoulders, the gorgeous curve of his biceps—his thighs as he climbed off the bike, his muscled ass. When I finally dragged my gaze back to his, his grin had eased into something a little more private—almost sultry. I'd been obviously checking him out. And he seemed to like it.

A thrill ran through me.

"Hey," I said, raising my phone demonstratively. "I was just about to call you."

"Yeah?" Priest asked. "Must've gotten the psychic message. I was hoping to run into you, too."

"I wanted to talk," I said.

"Me too." Priest climbed the stairs onto the porch, then placed a hand on my shoulder. The contact made my blood run hotter. "Come inside, we'll talk somewhere privately."

Blade caught my eye as Priest and I ascended the stairs, and he gave me a quick approving nod. He kept the rest of the members in the kitchen, busy with coffee and barbeque sandwiches, so that we'd have at least some privacy.

I led Priest down the hallway toward the door to my apartment, anticipation building in my gut. I know we'd said we weren't going to do anything about our attraction, and I didn't know where this conversation would take us, but I knew I was tired of living in the nebulous fog of the 'maybe'.

As I turned the corner toward my apartment, I saw the door was slightly ajar.

I paused. That was strange. I always locked my apartment door when I left—an old habit. Muscle memory, at this point, I never even noticed when I did it.

Had I forgotten to lock it this morning?

Well... forgetting to lock it was one thing. Leaving it open? That wasn't like me. The anticipatory thrill of talking with Priest—or maybe more—dissipated like steam, replaced with a dark sense of dread creeping through me.

"What is it?" Priest said from behind me.

"My door shouldn't be open," I said.

Before Priest could say anything, I stepped forward and pushed the door open, heart in my throat.

The room was empty—I was equal parts relieved and irritated, like part of me was hoping I'd find the culprit and it'd turn out to be a club member playing a trick on me. Or that I'd find who I suspected had actually done it in the act, so I could beat his ass the way he deserved.

My sheets were rumpled.

Disgust rose in my throat, sharp like bile.

Priest placed his hand gently at my lower back. "Something different?"

"I always make my bed," I said. God, I was uncomfortable here—my skin crawled like I could still feel Xavier's phantom presence. I knew it was him. There was no one else it would have been.

He'd been in my *bed.* What had he been doing? Lying in my sheets?

Jerking off?

I wanted to burn my whole fucking mattress.

"He was in my bed," I said coldly, and then cast my eyes around the room a little desperately, looking for other things that were different, or out of place. My gaze landed on the laundry hamper outside of the bathroom—the top of the wicker basket was tossed carelessly aside. I always kept it closed. Couldn't have my unwashed riding gear stinking up my bedroom. But now it was open.

I paced over.

Things were missing.

Nausea turned my stomach again. The clothes I'd worn yesterday—the t-shirt, the boxers, even the socks—were missing from the top of the laundry pile.

"He stole my fucking *clothes*." I whirled around and met Priest's eyes. He was pale with comprehension.

Priest leaned out of the bedroom door just enough to shout for Siren and Coop, and then approached me slowly. I was still standing over my laundry hamper, grimacing.

Priest gently wrapped his arms around my shoulders, tugging me flush against him, so my back was pressed against his chest. He took slow, deliberate breaths, and only then did I realize that my breaths were short and shallow with anxiety.

"I know it was him," I said. "I know it was Xavier."

"Yeah," Priest agreed, and his voice sounded low and dangerous in my ear. "We'll figure this out. I've got you."

The enforcers thundered up the stairs. I'd have to face the reality of this—explain what had happened right under our noses—in a few seconds, but I took a moment to close my eyes and lean heavily against the strength of Priest behind me. Only then did I realize how badly I needed it.

Chapter 12 - Priest

I held Mal close to my chest, intentionally breathing deeply in an attempt to get him to do the same. He was trembling, just enough that it was noticeable when he was pressed up against me like this.

The feeling sent an unfamiliar rage coursing through me. I'd dealt with a hell of a lot of shit during my years with Hell's Ankhor, but this was a new level of violation. Having someone sneak into our clubhouse? Into a member's *apartment*? It was so invasive, and honestly, it'd be easier to deal with if Xavier wanted something from the club. But he didn't—didn't want money, or gear, or recognition, or revenge. He just wanted *Mal.*

And that infuriated me. If Xavier thought he could just break in like this and steal from Mal—make him feel unsafe in his own home—he was going to pay.

I'd make sure of that.

Siren burst in through the door, with Coop hot on her heels. "What's going on?" she asked, a little panicked. "What happened?"

Mal pulled out of my hold then. Even in the midst of the anger and fear, I missed his warmth immediately. I didn't know how to fix this situation, but I did know that having him in my arms made it easier. But I also understood Mal didn't want to be seen so vulnerable in front of the enforcers—not yet. And from the way his expression hardened, the shock was wearing off, and was quickly being replaced by anger.

"Blade's still downstairs with the prospects," Coop said. "Need me to get him?"

"No, not now," Mal said. "I'll loop in him in later. Best to keep the prospects out of this as long as we can."

"Out of what?" Siren asked, glancing around the room like she was missing something.

"Someone broke in," I said.

Mal cringed and crossed his arms over his chest. Which only made me want to hold him again. "Not just someone," he admitted. "Xavier."

"Xavier?" Siren asked. "He was *in* the motel?"

"In my room," Mal said.

"What the fuck?" Coop asked. "Was he looking to steal shit?"

"He stole my clothes," Mal said, and the furrow in his brow deepened. "And he was in my bed."

"Gross," Coop said.

"Yeah," Mal said, sounding unimpressed. "*You* think it's fucking gross? Imagine how I feel. This is my fucking *space*. Now I have to think about that fucking creep poking around here when I'm not around? How did he even get *in?*"

"That's what we're going to figure out first," Siren said. "And figure out what all he stole. Coop, call the other enforcers and let them know what's up. I'm going to look around the motel for any signs of forced entry, and loop Blade into what's happening. He can decide what to do with the prospects."

I nodded. Siren was good at things like this—taking control. Making a plan. And that gave me more space to do what I wanted to do, which was make sure Mal was okay.

"All right," Mal said. "Thanks, Siren."

"That's why we're here," Siren said. "Holler if you find anything weird."

Mal and I both nodded, and then Siren and Coop stepped out of the bedroom, leaving Mal and me alone again.

Mal sighed heavily and scrubbed his hands over his face. "This is awful. God, I hate to think about him poking through all my stuff."

"Let's get it over with, then," I said, and ran my hand soothingly over the width of his shoulders. "I'll follow your lead."

If I were in his position, I wouldn't want anyone else sniffing around my things. I just wanted to be here to support him—in whatever way I could. Whatever way he'd let me.

"If he went for the dirty laundry, maybe he went for the clean stuff, too," Mal grumbled. He checked in his drawers and found them mostly undisturbed. With a sigh of relief, he moved to the nightstand and began opening those drawers. Then he stilled, his face falling.

"What is it?" I asked.

"Yeah, he was in here," Mal muttered, picking carefully through the drawer. I stepped closer and peered over his shoulder.

It was exactly the kind of drawer I'd expect to find in a guy's nightstand—hell, mine looked the same for many years of my life. Condoms, lube, a smattering of toys—was that a cock ring?—and other detritus like tissues and wet wipes. But then Mal stilled. His head turned, his gaze toward the bed. I followed his line of sight.

On the mattress, lying in the rumpled sheets, was another toy. A *big* toy. It was a dildo, black, ridged, curved—not realistic to a real cock, just made to feel good. The base was big, too—not just the standard flared base. It looked like it took batteries. Did it *vibrate?*

I was staring. I knew I shouldn't be staring, but I was staring.

It was so inappropriate, especially given the circumstances, but my brain conjured the images before I could stop them. Mal, spread out on his big bed, muffling his moans into his forearm as his other hand worked the huge toy into his tight hole. Did he have a certain way he liked it? Did he know how to make the toy hit is prostate just right? Or was it only for special occasions?

God, I bet he looked amazing, head tilted back, heels digging into the mattress, toes curling, a sheen of sweat across his gorgeous skin—

I blinked hard and pushed those thoughts away. I did *not* need to be getting hard—or even thinking this way—when we were dealing with a stalker who had broken in.

Except... toys hadn't really been a part of my sex life with Ankh. I didn't have *any* experience with them, really. But Mal clearly did. Was he into using them with partners? Would he let *me* work the toy into him until he screamed?

Fuck. *Fuck.* I needed to focus.

A little curl of guilt flared in my gut alongside the arousal. Not only because I was getting horny for Mal while we were searching his room, but because of the way my thoughts had immediately gone to Ankh, too. And it hadn't hurt. Should it have?

Would I think about Ankh every time I thought about a relationship with Mal? Was that wrong? Was it unfair to Mal?

Was it unfair to Ankh?

I wanted to do right by them both—but I was confused, lost in the mess of my own desire and guilt. I'd have to work it out later. There were more important things at hand now. Mal needed me—I couldn't be stuck in my own head.

"Don't look so shocked," Mal said, gently teasing, then knocked his elbow into my ribs. From the slight flush in his cheeks, he had some idea of where my mind went. "I'm more concerned about if he *used* it."

I wrinkled my nose at the implication. "That's disgusting," I said. "You'll have to replace it. I'll approve the request to use club funds."

Mal laughed and swatted at me, and my mood lifted to see him smiling again, despite what he was dealing with.

Then, in the hallway, footsteps pounded up the stairs—a *lot* of footsteps. Mal cringed, pulling the sheets over the dildo, and we stepped apart. There was a knock at the door, and then Raven stuck his head inside. "Pop? Mal? Are you okay?"

"Yeah, son, we're fine," I said. "Why are you here? Coop was supposed to call the enforcers."

"I was with Gunnar," Raven said. "Cavalry's here. Blade's still with the prospects."

He stepped inside, with Gunnar, Rebel, and Tru behind him, and then Siren and Coop walked back in, as well. Mal tensed again, and I placed a hand on his shoulder. Surely having all these people in his room wasn't helping him feel more in control—but we had to work together to get to the bottom of this.

"He take anything else that you noticed?" Siren asked.

I glanced at Mal questioningly, silently asking with my eyebrows raised if he wanted me to do the talking. He just shook his head, then sighed. "No, it looks like he only took my dirty laundry."

Cringes from the enforcers.

"And it looks like he snooped around a lot of things, in my nightstand and my dresser, but I didn't notice anything else missing."

"I want to call this in, Mal," Rebel said. "To the station. He broke the restraining order."

"We don't have any definitive proof that it was him, though," Mal said through gritted teeth. "Even though I know in my gut it was."

"That's why we gotta get the cops involved," Rebel said. "I'll have the guys look for any fingerprints or other traces that could tie it back to Xavier. He's in the system, so if he's left something behind, we'll find it. And since you already have the restraining order in place, they'll do a thorough search."

Mal nodded, and Rebel stepped outside to put the call in.

"Did you find any evidence of how he got in?" I asked Siren.

"No," she said with a sigh. "Everything looks to be normal."

"That's what I was discussing with Tru on the way here," Raven said. "We need to get the motel security up to the same standards as the clubhouse. Cameras, for one thing. A better alarm system."

"Right," Tru said. "I know the Junee chapter doesn't have as much history of trouble as the Elkin Lake guys, but now that we're part of the same crew, we need to bring the motel up to the same standards. This isn't going to be the last time something like this happens."

Gunnar nodded in agreement. "And I think if we want to prevent it from happening again, we need to send a message."

"What exactly does that mean?" I asked with my eyebrows raised.

"We need to track Xavier down," Gunnar said with his eyes narrowed. "*Now*. Before this escalates. I think this is overdue for some club justice."

"No," Mal said. "We're not there yet."

"You don't think so?" Gunnar asked. "He broke into your *home*, Mal."

"I know," Mal said. "But we've already got the restraining order in. If he gets knocked around, that's not going to reflect well on the club."

Gunnar sighed and crossed his arms over his chest. "It wouldn't be traced back to us."

"Maybe not," Mal said, "and I'm not saying he doesn't deserve it. But let's get the cops in here first and see if we can't get him dealt with through legal channels."

I nodded in agreement. "But this *is* serious escalation. If he got in and we can't figure out how—that's seriously dangerous. He's a danger to us, regardless of how he looks."

"That's right," Tru said. "We have to make sure something like this doesn't happen again. Who knows what he would've done if Mal was here when he broke in."

I cringed at the thought, then turned to Mal. "He's right. This could've gone a lot differently."

Mal sighed and rubbed at his eyes. "All right, guys, can we continue this conversation downstairs? I'm kind of over having people in my apartment right now."

"Sure," Raven said. "Come on, everyone, let's put some coffee on."

"I'll catch up Blade and the prospects," Gunnar said. The enforcers left the room, leaving Priest and me alone again.

Mal sighed deeply. He glanced at his bed like he wanted to sit down—but then cringed at the state of the sheets and leaned against the wall instead. "This is such a shit show."

I stepped closer again, then placed my hand on his shoulder. Some of the tension eased in his posture, and he glanced gratefully at me.

"Thanks," he said.

"For what?" I asked. I hadn't done much today, other than stand at his back and get wrapped up in my inappropriate thoughts about his toys.

"For being here," Mal said. "This... this is a lot."

"Pack some stuff," I said. "You don't need to stay here tonight."

"What?" Mal asked. "That's not necessary."

"I have to put my foot down on this one, Mal," I said. "It's not safe for you to be here—at least not until we get the security kicked up substantially."

And I wasn't just saying that because I wanted Mal closer to me, where I could protect him should Xavier show his face again. It just made sense. If Xavier was unstable, who knows how he'd react if he came across a member of the club in the motel while he was prowling?

Mal looked at me and ducked his chin with a slight nod. "You're right."

I huffed a laugh. "Honestly, I expected you to fight me on this."

He glanced around the room. "I really don't want to stay here," he admitted. "Knowing he was in here. In my *bed*."

"I'll get Raven to strip the sheets for you, if that's okay?"

"Yeah. Yeah, that'll work." Mal nodded decisively, then pushed off the wall to start gathering his things. "It'll be fine."

He glanced at me with his brow furrowed, like he wasn't sure if that was true. I wanted so badly to pull him into my arms again, kiss the back of his neck and tell him there wasn't a way in hell I was going to let Xavier anywhere near him again. But he didn't need me to act like his—his *partner*. Right now, he needed me to step up as vice president. And that I knew how to do.

"It will be," I said with a serious nod. "I'll make sure of it."

Chapter 13 - Mal

It took a couple hours to get all our ducks in a row at the motel. I packed my things best I could, and the other club members arranged other places to stay, the Elkin Lake clubhouse or with family or partners, as well. That made me feel a little better about crashing at the clubhouse— made me feel like this endeavor was less about me. Even if I knew it was a pain in the ass for everyone in the club, and knew it was, at least partially, my fault.

I climbed off my bike outside the Elkin Lake clubhouse, tugged off my helmet, and paused as I began to untie my duffel from the pannier over the back wheel.

Star, Eli, and Nix were laughing as they walked up the stairs to the clubhouse front porch, bags in hand. They didn't seem to be too bothered by being displaced from their apartments, but I still felt guilty. I shouldn't have ignored Xavier for so long. I was the damn co-president and I'd gotten cocky, thinking I could handle it. And now the entire club was paying the price.

"Hey," Priest said, hurrying down the porch stairs. He'd left the motel before me, saying he needed to ensure the empty rooms were fit to have visitors. Just another pang of guilt for me, too, giving Priest extra work to do. Still, even after spending only a few hours apart, I was relieved to see him. His expression softened with concern as he approached. "Everything okay?"

"Yeah," I said, then set my teeth into my lower lip thoughtfully. "Just a little pissed."

"At Xavier? Hell, yeah, you should be."

"No, no," I said. "At myself."

Priest tilted his head curiously. "You know this isn't your fault."

"You can't say that," I said with a self-deprecating laugh. "I was the one who blew off Xavier's harassment in the first place, even as it became worse and more frequent. Hell, you had to convince me even he was even a threat at all!"

"That still doesn't make it your fault," Priest said. "You were trying to keep your business private. No one blames you for that."

"I know they don't," I said. "But my actions have uprooted some of our members, Priest. We're not safe in our own home."

His hand fell to my shoulder. He'd been doing that a lot recently—touching my shoulder, or the middle of my back. It was such a gentle, grounding gesture. One that I was beginning to rely on a lot.

"I know it doesn't look like much," I said, "it's not as fancy as the clubhouse, sure, but—it's home. It's *my* home. I raised Dante there. Our entire club made it our home. And the thought that I've uprooted my family just because of some dumb hookup—" I cringed and toed at the dirt. "Some president."

"Yeah," Priest said. "I understand."

I paused. I'd expected Priest to huff and puff and reiterate that I was doing just fine—the way Blade would. But Priest just smiled, his hand still on my shoulder.

"I know what it's like to feel like you're letting the club down," he said, quietly. "Feeling like you missed something—let something slip through the cracks, and now everyone else has to pay for your oversight."

Something in my chest felt like it was cracking open. "Yeah. Yeah, it's exactly that. How could I have missed this? How could I have not seen this coming?"

"We can't do it all, as much as we try," Priest said. "We're always going to make mistakes. Part of the gig. And, all things considered, this one is pretty manageable so far."

"So far," I said. It was still a relief to hear it, though—not someone telling me that I was still a good president, but Priest telling me that, yeah, this was a mistake, but it was one we'd recover from.

"And honestly," Priest said, "the motel *is* overdue for a security upgrade. But you know we weren't going to get around to it until something like this happened."

I barked a surprised laugh. "Well, you're not wrong about that."

Then, Priest moved his hand from my shoulder, but only to swing his arm around me and tug me in for a rough, hard hug.

"Do you really want to spend the night in one of those guest rooms?" he asked with a grin.

"Honestly? Not looking forward to it," I admitted.

"Come on," he said. "Crash at my place again."

Before I could answer, Priest was deftly unfastening my duffel from the pannier and swinging it over his shoulder. He quirked an eyebrow at me.

He really *did* understand how I felt about this whole situation—the messy mix of guilt and embarrassment and desire to improve. To serve the club as best I could—to not let them get dragged into my mistakes and failures. I didn't have to explain it, and he knew he didn't need to reassure me that I was a capable president.

The foundation of our lives was the same. There was so much I didn't have to explain. There was so much textured history between us, rich and unspoken—something that had taken decades to build. Something I wouldn't be able to build with someone new from scratch, not at this stage of my life.

"All right," I said. "If you insist."

Priest nodded, smiling, and led me down the path to his cabin. He was still carrying my duffel.

I was glad I wasn't going to be subjected to the worried doting of my members, but at the same time, I was nervous to spend another night at Priest's. It didn't mean anything, other than the fact that Priest was worried about me and wanted me to be able to sleep comfortably. Right?

But he was carrying my duffel, the way someone might when they were trying to impress a date.

God, I felt like a confused teenager instead of a grown man pushing fifty-five. The break-in had thrown a wrench into everything I'd planned to discuss with Priest about what was going on between us. It felt less urgent now—we had bigger things to sort out. The club came first. And yet the confusion of the tension and attraction between us weighed on me. In my gut I knew I wanted more from Priest. Wanted his kiss, his hands on me, his warm comforting voice in my ear sighing out moans when he came.

But there was so much baggage there, too—and not just the duffel swung over his shoulder. The roles we had to play, the pain of Ankh's loss, the twist of fear in my chest when I considered what might happen if this fell apart the way things had fallen apart with Melanie.

It made my head hurt. More than anything, I needed some good sleep.

Priest led me across the threshold to his cabin and set my duffel gently on the floor.

"Thanks," I said, glancing around the now-familiar, cozy space. "I'll sleep better on this couch than I would on one of those old twin mattresses, that's for sure."

From the kitchen, Priest laughed. "Might be due for an upgrade on those, too."

I moved my duffel to the couch with some resignation. What had I expected? For Priest to say no, of course you won't be on the couch, and then corral me into his bedroom? That'd be ridiculous, and foolish. But I couldn't help my disappointment at the prospect of a night on the couch, regardless of how comfortable it was.

I cleared my throat.

Silence stretched between us.

Priest opened the fridge. "Need a nightcap?"

"Yeah," I said immediately. "Yeah, that sounds great."

Priest cracked two cans of beer and handed me one. I took a sip, grateful for the chill of the liquid and, honestly, to have something to do with my hands. Then Priest lingered behind the couch, like he wasn't sure if he should stay and talk or disappear into his bedroom. And I wasn't sure what I wanted, either. God, today had been a mess. Really what I needed was a little bit of time to clear my head.

"Do you mind if I take a quick shower?" I asked. "Kind of want to get the itchy feeling off."

The feeling of being violated—of feeling like Xavier's hands were still on me.

"Oh!" Priest said, shaking his head like he was surprised with himself. "Yes, sorry, I should've offered. Here, come on, there's just the one upstairs, but it's nice."

Right. The guest bathroom was a half-bath—no shower. I hadn't considered that when I asked, and part of me wanted to rescind the request, but that'd only make things more awkward.

I grabbed a change of clothes from my bag and followed Priest up the stairs to his bedroom. I tried not to be nosy and peek around his room too much, but I couldn't resist taking in what I could: his rumpled ivory sheets, a cozy-looking red flannel quilt, candles on the dresser, an upturned novel and abandoned mug on the nightstand, leather jacket hanging off the doorknob to the closet.

I wanted to spend more time in this room. Wanted to fall into the sheets with him like I belonged there.

"Clean towels are under the sink. Take your time. And enjoy the shower beer," Priest said with a laugh.

"It's just what I need," I said, matching his grin.

The master bath was simple, but with elements of luxury that showed how much care the guys had put into building the cabin: a rainfall-style showerhead, big shower stall with clear glass doors, and black countertop with Priest's razor and toothbrush. I turned the water on as hot as it could go, undressed and climbed under the spray.

And then I realized I hadn't brought any of my toiletries.

Not a huge problem—I popped open Priest's body wash. Surely, he wouldn't mind me using some.

And god, it smelled good. Subtle, like Priest smelled, a hint of citrus and something rich and woodsy. Arousal curled in my gut, in an instinctive, animal way. Something about smelling like him made me dizzy with desire, and it only got worse as I ran the soap over my arms and chest in a luxurious lather. And maybe I went a little slower than I might usually, savoring the rich, familiar smell as it filled the shower, as the steam and the hot water loosened my tense muscles.

I closed my eyes as I ran my hands over my chest again. Immediately, I thought of Priest—how could I not, with his scent surrounding me, knowing he spent time in this same shower, naked and wet, using the same soap I was using? And for once, I didn't try to push the thoughts away.

Priest had looked so surprised to see the toy on my bed. I'd been embarrassed at first, because I knew it wasn't exactly a beginner's toy. It was big, the way I liked it, and it hit all the right places inside me. It'd been a long time since I had a regular partner, and sometimes I just wanted to be *fucked*. I'd expected that Priest would be awkward, or pretend he hadn't seen it, but when I'd risked a glance over at him, his face had looked... interested.

Curious.

Maybe even turned on.

His eyes had widened a little, and his mouth had dropped open. A flush had built in his cheeks. Had he been thinking about me using it?

The thought made the arousal burn even hotter inside me. My cock began to fill with interest, and I skated my hand up and down my chest, over the plane of my abs.

Had he been thinking about using it on me?

I bit back a groan. The fantasy slammed into my mind, fully formed like it'd just been waiting for me to acknowledge it. I imagined myself spread out on Priest's bed, on my back with my knees bent, with Priest kneeling at my side. He'd be good at touching me, too—gentle but strong. Practiced. He'd press one hand into the center of my chest, pinning me down, as he pushed the lube-slick dildo inside me.

Fuck, it'd feel even better that way, the familiar shape inside me so thick and hard, but with Priest's hands directing it. He'd fuck me slow and deep, pressing it all the way into the base, and then dragging it out slowly. Making me beg for it, not like the hard and fast way I fucked myself.

I wrapped my hand around my cock. It only took a few strokes, with my hand slick with his body wash, to bring myself to full hardness. I braced one hand on the wall and tipped my head forward, letting the water thrum across the tense back of my neck and the width of my shoulders.

Did Priest run his mouth in bed? God, I hoped he did. I tightened my grip around my cock as I imagined Priest leaning down, keeping me pinned to the bed, refusing to touch my cock as he fucked me with the toy. He'd whisper into my ear, in that low, familiar voice, telling me how good I was doing. How he wanted to see me come. How he'd give me his cock if I took the toy well enough.

Fuck. My knees felt weak, unstable; my abs tensed as the heat in my gut burned hotter and curled tighter. My hand moved quickly up and down the length of my cock. I couldn't resist the pleasure of it, couldn't hold it off. It was too overwhelming, with his scent all around me and the fantasy so intense in my imagination.

I imagined Priest withdrawing the toy, then gripping my thighs with both hands, pressing me backward—folding me in half—and sliding his hot, hard cock inside me with no resistance. It'd feel so much better than the toy, so fucking hot and *real,* like I hadn't felt in such a long time. He'd groan as he did so, leaning forward to capture my lips in a sloppy, sexy kiss, fucking his tongue into my mouth the same way he fucked his cock into my ass.

I gasped, working my hand fast and hard as my orgasm crested. My hand scrabbled at the shower wall as my body shuddered. The pleasure raced through me with an intensity I wasn't used to—at home, my orgasms were pretty perfunctory, at this point. But the fantasy was so real, so intense, and I wanted Priest *so* fucking badly—it shocked me how badly I wanted him. I came in ropes onto the shower wall, and before I could remember where I was, a loud, low groan slipped through my lips, echoing through Priest's big, fancy bathroom.

And then the fucking door burst open.

"Are you all right?" Priest asked in a high, shocked tone. "I heard something—"

"Holy shit!" I nearly shouted. I was completely visible through the glass doors of the shower, from my hand on my dick to the cum on his shower wall. My face flamed hot and I tried to turn away in such a hurry—would rather show my ass than my dick—that my feet slipped in the soapy water.

I fell flat on my ass, nearly braining myself on the tile but catching myself at the last minute. It was only the size of the shower stall that saved me from concussing myself— but my foot did almost take out one of the little shelves in the corner. Almost.

"Fuck," I groaned. So much for luxuriating in the aftermath of my orgasm. I rubbed my hand over my face, and—oh, come on, there was still soap on my hand, and it got in my eyes. "Fuck!" I said, wriggling around on the shower floor until I got my face under the shower spray, then I tilted my head back underneath it to rinse the soap out of my eyes.

Priest cleared his throat. "Um."

Oh, so he was still standing in the bathroom watching all this. Great. I didn't open my eyes.

"This is your fault," I grumbled.

"Here's a towel," Priest said, and I heard the shower door open. I shut off the water, then reached out blindly until my hand met the fluffy towel.

I wiped off my face first, then staggered to my feet and wrapped the towel around my waist with my back to Priest. Facing the wall, I pressed my lips together and tried to will my cheeks from burning too hot. This was so embarrassing. It was embarrassing enough to get caught jerking off, but then nearly destroying his shower, too? And my whole body ached from the fall—it made me feel old. Like if I'd landed a little differently on my ass, we'd be calling the ambulance to come haul me back to my feet.

But I couldn't just stand in the shower grimacing and hoping that Priest would leave, because he wouldn't. Wasn't his style. So I squared my shoulders and turned around.

Priest did not look even the slightest bit concerned. Actually, his warm blue eyes were glittering with laughter, and he was biting his lower lip to try to hide a grin. Even his shoulders were quivering, like it was taking all his self-control to not double over.

Suddenly, my humiliation was washed away.

"Come on," I said with a dramatic eyeroll. I slugged him on the shoulder as I walked past, holding the towel up around my waist and dripping all over the floor. "Shouldn't you be apologizing to me?"

"Sorry, old man, did you break a hip in there?" Priest said, and then broke down laughing.

"I *could've*!" I said with a huff. "I was having a moment!"

"Sounds like it," Priest teased. "I thought you were *hurt*."

"Well, I am now." I leaned against the bathroom counter. "Was having a nice time before that."

"Looked like it," Priest said. He leaned against the counter at my side and knocked his shoulder against mine. "Sorry. Just kind of on edge with everything that's going on."

"What, did you think Xavier was hiding in the bathroom somehow?"

"Maybe!" Priest threw his hands up. "I wasn't really thinking. I just acted."

"Well, thanks for trying to save my life," I said with a fond shake of my head. "I'm super relaxed now."

Priest grinned sheepishly, then peered over his shoulder and grabbed the beer I'd left on the counter. "Hey, at least this survived the chaos," he said, and pressed it into my hand.

I took a grateful swig and then shook my head. "Hell of a way to end a hell of a day."

"Can't say it was boring, at least," Priest said. "I'll let you get changed. Sorry again about that."

"Don't worry about it," I said with a grin. "Gotta keep things interesting somehow."

Priest slipped out of the bathroom, leaving me to towel off and change into my pajamas. I was still embarrassed, but it wasn't that big of a deal, was it? Maybe the attraction I felt for him was new, but it was still *Priest*. One of my oldest friends. A guy who could see me fall flat on my ass buck naked and laugh at me for it. It was easy being with him—comfortable, even in moments like this.

And in that comfort, my desire didn't scare me quite as much anymore. It was just Priest. Even if things went south, there wasn't anything that could shatter our decades-long friendship.

I didn't have to have all the answers, but I was starting to think that maybe we could figure things out together.

Chapter 14 - Priest

After a few minutes of knocking around in the bathroom, Mal stepped into my room with a sheepish, embarrassed grin on his face. Despite the chaos just a few minutes prior, he looked good, relaxed in an old pair of sweatpants and threadbare t-shirt that clung to the curve of his pecs and hugged the swell of his biceps. As he stepped across the threshold, he grimaced and rubbed at his hip.

"Damn, you really fell hard, didn't you?" I stood up from where I'd been sitting on the edge of the bed and set my hand at his waist to steady him.

"Come on now, do you think I'm gonna fall again?" Mal asked, laughing as he swatted my hand away. "I'm not *that* old."

I laughed, but as Mal headed toward the stairs, I caught his wrist. "Come on, I'm not making you sleep on the couch after that fall."

"It's fine—"

"It's a comfortable couch," I interrupted, "but it's not *that* comfortable. You're in here tonight."

"That's not—"

"I insist," I said with a smile. "This bad boy is a California king, there's plenty of space."

Sure, there were beds available in the clubhouse—but Mal didn't need to be walking that distance if his hip was bothering him where he'd fallen, and those mattresses were like jail cell beds compared to the luxury of my big new bed. He wouldn't get any good rest anywhere else.

And, selfishly, I wanted him close to me after the stress of the day.

Mal shook his head, grinning, but didn't push back again. He eased into the bed, still on top of the covers, and leaned against the headboard. I finished getting ready for bed, taking my turn in the bathroom, brushing my teeth with the door open. I felt Mal's eyes on me the whole time, but it wasn't uncomfortable.

Sure, I'd been stunned speechless when I'd burst into the bathroom. And maybe it'd been unreasonable to panic like I had, but the violation of having Xavier break into the motel was still so fresh in my mind. I'd immediately jumped to insane conclusions, thinking that Xavier had somehow gotten a camera into the bathroom, or something like that. Of course it made no sense—why would it be in *my* house?—but I was starting to realize that when it came to Mal, my logic was malfunctioning.

I'd been frozen by surprise when I saw Mal—and also by the whiplash of terror turning into arousal. Mal had looked so fucking hot as he came, muscles tensing and his hand wrapped around his hard, thick cock.

Knowing he was doing that in *my* shower made it even hotter.

And then he'd fallen on his ass. The image made me grin around my toothbrush. Thankfully, he wasn't hurt, and, admittedly, it was fucking hilarious. Laughing it about it together felt so natural, immediately alleviating any awkwardness or embarrassment between us. It didn't feel right to send him downstairs to the couch after that. That'd be a falsehood—pretending that whatever was between us *wasn't* between us. And I was getting too old to play games like that.

I knew better than to make that decision for Mal, though. Even if he looked comfortable, lounging on the bed, I didn't want to make assumptions.

I set my toothbrush aside and stepped out of the bathroom. "Hey," I said as I stripped my shirt over my head, leaving me in just my sweatpants to sleep, "do you want me to take the couch?"

Mal's eyes tracked over my bare chest. "Uh. No, of course not. It's your bed." He cleared his throat. "And like you said, it's big enough."

It'd been my idea, but suddenly the idea of sharing a bed with Mal made anxiety curl in my gut. We couldn't sleep side by side in my bed, pretending we were still just friends, pretending things were normal. The tension between us was too far gone. It meant we'd have to address the conversation we were supposed to have in Mal's room, before we'd been sidetracked by Xavier's mess.

But god, I wanted to sleep next to Mal. I longed to have another warm body in my big, cold bed—and I wanted *him* beside me, specifically.

So I steeled myself and crawled into the bed beside him. The mattress was big enough that there was plenty of space between us, and yet I wanted to roll closer, tug him into my arms, press his back to my chest and kiss his nape. The intensity of that want was… still surprising, but not unfamiliar, at this point. I shut off the light and turned on my side toward him; Mal turned the other way and I took a moment to admire the broad plane of his back.

The silence lingered, but from the pace of Mal's breathing, I knew he was still awake.

"Hey," I murmured.

Mal rolled over, turning toward me. Even in the dark room, having his gaze on me was simultaneously soothing and exciting.

"What are we doing here?" I asked.

Mal smiled, only a little hesitantly. "Kind of overdue for this conversation, huh?"

"Yeah," I said. "We're a little too old to be beating around the bush like this, don't you think?"

"And we've seen it happen a few too many times," Mal said teasingly.

"God, don't remind me," I said. "Gunnar and Raven drove me crazy dancing around each other."

"They were still learning at that age," Mal said. "Hadn't had the experience we've got."

"I know, I know," I said. "Still. They could've benefited from a conversation like this a little earlier."

"What kind of conversation *is* this?" Mal asked.

I pressed my lips together. That was a good question— what did I need to tell him? What did I want to know? What did I want us to *be?*

Mal must've sensed my uncertainty, because he huffed a laugh and said, "I'll go first. I was intending to have this conversation earlier, anyway." He paused and took a breath, but then a smile spread across his face. "So, I've been having these dreams."

"Dreams?" I raised my eyebrows. "*Good* dreams, I hope."

Mal bit his lower lip. "Yeah, they're good dreams. About you. And—and I mean, it's pretty obvious there's... something between us."

"I've been having dreams, too," I admitted, even as my face flushed. "Makes me feel like I'm in my twenties again."

"I'm attracted to you," Mal said unashamedly. "Pretty powerfully. But—I don't want to overstep any boundaries, you know? Our friendship comes first. Our club comes first."

God, he was such a good man. The obvious concern in his eyes made me feel comfortable talking about my hesitations—he obviously wouldn't take it as a personal slight against himself.

"Obviously, I'm attracted to you, too," I acknowledged, and even though it was, to me, obvious, Mal's eyes still widened like he hadn't expected me to say it. "But I'm still feeling a little... at sea about it, I guess. I don't know what we should do. I don't know what I'm comfortable with."

Mal nodded, but said nothing, silently encouraging me to continue.

"I feel so comfortable with you. But..." I paused as my tongue tripped over the words. It wasn't quite embarrassing to admit it, but it was... vulnerable. I'd never thought it'd be something I'd have to tell anyone else. Mal deserved to know, though. Deserved to know why this was so challenging for me. "I haven't been with anyone since Ankh. I mean—before or after. He was my first, and I thought he'd be my only."

Mal's eyes softened, and he reached out, then folded one hand over mind.

"I still love him, even though he's gone," I said. "And—and I know I always will. I haven't wanted anyone since his death. Until now. And sometimes I get caught up in my head, thinking—should I be feeling this way? Is it too soon?"

Something inside my chest twisted, sudden and painful. It was the first time I'd voiced those thoughts, and it incited a mixture of pain, guilt, and relief at finally *saying* it. I hadn't even meant to say that much, but it was so easy to talk to Mal, what with years of history between us, and the fact that he knew Ankh nearly as well as I did.

"I don't mean to dump all this on you," I said.

Mal scooted a little closer on the mattress, and kept his hand folded over mine.

"I understand," he said. "I thought about that too, when all this... started. The last thing I want is to try to replace Ankh. I know that's impossible—and it's not something I would ever want." Mal sighed. "He was my friend, too."

Only when they eased did I realize how tense my shoulders had been. "It's hard being without him."

"Yeah," Mal agreed. "And—you may have noticed this, but I don't have a whole lot of experience in the serious-relationships field."

I snorted, grateful for a little bit of lightheartedness. "Yeah, I've noticed that."

"I don't think either of us want to jump into anything serious. At least, *I'm* definitely not ready to commit to anything serious. But... what's the point of avoiding what's between us?" Mal asked. "We're responsible adults, as far as I can tell."

"Most of the time," I agreed. "So...what are you saying?"

Mal smiled warmly. "We're attracted to each other. We're good friends—we trust each other. We *respect* each other. I think we're both capable of talking about what we want—and need. Without having it become such a huge deal."

I nodded in agreement. "That sounds right."

"So maybe we should just...try it and see where things go," Mal said. "You don't need to worry about me trying to replace Ankh—or getting jealous of what you two had together. And I'm not going to pressure you for anything more than what you want. No hard feelings. I think we both deserve a chance to feel good, you know?"

It sounded so simple when he put it like that. "Taking care of each other," I said.

"Exactly," Mal agreed. "We're friends first. We know best how to take care of each other."

"Yeah," I said. Having Mal this close to me was making me dizzy with desire—here, in my dark room, in my bed, Mal was telling me he wanted to *take care* of me. He understood what I felt for Ankh—and how this was different.

And I wanted it. I wanted *him.*

"Yeah," I repeated. "Yeah, I want that."

Mal reached out and set his hand at the slight curve of my waist, then leaned in close. He didn't close the distance between us, though, just lingered close enough that I could feel his warm breath ghosting over my lips.

He was letting me decide. He wanted me to be the one to close the distance—giving me another chance to change my mind. He was so *kind.* Gratitude warmed my chest, alongside the heat of arousal low in my gut as I leaned forward and pressed my lips to his.

To start, it was a barely there touch of lips. God, it'd been so long since I'd been kissed that I couldn't hold back my surprised inhale at the contact. It made my lips part, which deepened the kiss; Mal caught my lower lip between his and sucked gently. Oh, I wanted more of that—more of *him.* I reached blindly for him, fisting my hand in the front of his shirt to tug him closer. I tangled our legs together, opened my mouth wider, and Mal chuckled into the kiss at my sudden passion.

He stopped laughing as I deepened the kiss even more, though. I slid my other hand under the hem of his shirt, skating over the defined ridge of his abs, as I slipped my tongue into his mouth. He kissed well, hot and demanding with an edge of teeth, and as we traded sloppy kisses back and forth, my desire only increased. God, I wanted him. It felt as if every nerve in my body was suddenly reawakened after years of numbness. Mal's hands and his mouth sent tingles racing across my skin, and I moaned into the kiss as I tried to pull him even closer.

"God, *Priest,*" Mal groaned as he slid his hand from my waist to my ass, then dug his fingers into the muscle. The sensation made me gasp.

I broke the kiss, but only to exhale hard against his jaw, savoring the scratch of his slight beard. "Wow," I said, a little breathlessly.

"Wow what?" Mal asked. He tipped his head back, his hand still kneading at my ass.

"Didn't know I could still feel like this," I admitted. I kissed his neck.

Mal sighed. "Pretty good, right?"

"I feel like a goddamn teenager," I said, then smiled against his skin.

"I'm *that* good, huh?" Mal teased.

"Or I'm that desperate," I joked back.

"Doubting my skills?" Mal asked with a grin.

Then in one swift movement, he put his hands on my shoulders and pinned me flat to the mattress. He kissed me hard and passionately, taking control easily. I was used to being the one in control in situations like this, but there was nothing about sex with Mal that I was used to. He fucked his tongue deep into my mouth as he got both hands under my shirt, pressing firmly over my abs and then up to my pecs, teasing my nipples.

"Not doubting," I managed to gasp out between kisses. "*Fuck*, that feels good."

Mal grinned then pulled away just enough to wrestle my shirt off and over my head. He sat up, straddling my hips, and I groaned as his ass pressed against my hard cock. Mal gazed down at me with a soft look in his eyes, as he trailed one hand over my chest.

I flushed under the intensity of his gaze, gripping his thighs as I squirmed a little underneath him. "Come on," I muttered.

"What?" Mal asked. He grinned, looking suddenly predatory—it made my cock throb against his ass. "Shy?"

"It's just been a while," I said. "Not used to being looked at."

"*Admired* is a better word," Mal said, low. "You're so fucking hot it makes me crazy."

He said it with such seriousness that I almost believed him. I'd never had a *new* partner—part of me thrilled at the unfamiliarity, even if I felt a little vulnerable and exposed, too.

Mal leaned down again, then shifted so his body was lying flat on top of mine, our bare chests pressed together. His body was so firm and hot against mine, the weight of him drove any unsure thoughts from my mind as he kissed me again.

"Can I blow you?" he asked against my mouth.

Well, there went my brain. I'd thought we'd just roll around a bit, make out like teenagers, but now the thought of having Mal's mouth on my dick made my whole body light up with desire.

I must've taken too long to answer, because Mal said, "Or not. Whatever you want."

"Fuck, yes, yes, please," I said hurriedly.

"Yeah?" Mal pulled away, smiling.

"You want to?" I asked, still a little shocked.

"Been dreaming about it," Mal admitted. Then he began to move down my body, dropping kisses on my shoulder, collarbone, chest, abs, moving down, down, down. I tried not to shift too restlessly on the mattress as he teased me, but it felt so dizzyingly good. I clutched at the sheets. Finally, he settled between my spread legs and mouthed wet kisses at my hip, just over the waistband of my sweatpants. My cock was so fucking hard it hurt.

Mal glanced up and grinned at me, apparently getting a kick out of how wrecked I was just from his teasing kisses. He gripped my cock through my sweatpants, and I gasped at the contact. Even with the cotton between his hand and my skin, it felt amazing—tight pressure sending a zing of intense pleasure up my spine. I let go of the sheets only to grip his shoulders instead. If I didn't ground myself with that touch, I might float the fuck away.

"Nice," Mal murmured, impressed, and then tugged my sweatpants down without preamble. He didn't pull them off, just tugged them down enough to free my hard cock, which slapped against my belly. I moaned at the sudden sensation of being exposed, but before I had a chance to feel self-conscious, Mal had his hand on my cock. He gave me a few lazy, curious strokes, and my toes curled against the sheets.

I felt like I hadn't been touched in a century. I'd gotten so used to the feeling of my own hand, jerking myself in a perfunctory way for the physical release, not because I felt any real desire. Mal's hand on me sent pleasure roaring through me, and I threw my head back and moaned, low and loud.

Before I could look back down, though, Mal replaced his hand with his mouth.

I gasped again as my world narrowed to the sensation of his mouth on my cock. He gripped the base of my cock in hand and sucked hard at the head—the white-hot pleasure made me grip his nape hard. He didn't waste any more time teasing me, though. He slid his mouth down my length, until his lips met his fist, and then slowly dragged back up, moving his hand as well so I was never without sensation.

"Mmh," he murmured after pulling off my cock with a wet pop. "Tastes good."

"Christ, Mal," I managed to say around my heaving breaths.

He shot me a wicked smile, and then sucked me into his mouth again. This time, he moved quickly, overwhelming me with heat and suction. The pleasure traveled from the crown of my head all the way to my toes, and I hooked one leg around Mal's waist, desperate to have him as close as possible.

"Not gonna last," I said. "Fuck, Mal, that's good."

Mal just hummed around my cock in acknowledgment, and the vibrations made my eyes roll back. I'd expected him to pull off and finish me with his hands, but apparently that wasn't Mal's plan. He just kept sucking me hard and fast, and the wet heat drew me closer and closer to the edge. The hot desire I'd felt all night intensified low in my hips, coiling like a spring.

"Fuck, fuck," I groaned, with one hand still on his nape and the other at his shoulder.

He took me deep into his mouth, as far as he could go, nearly into his throat. I moaned, low and long as I tumbled over the edge. My orgasm raced through me, and my back arched off the bed as I came down his throat. It was more intense than I'd had in years. Mal worked me through the aftershocks, dragging his tongue over my cock until I tugged desperately at his nape, groaning and oversensitive.

I sprawled pliant on the bed. My mind felt like it was running on half-speed, and my entire body was loose and lazy with pleasure.

"That was amazing," I said, and my voice was scratchy and fucked-out even to my own ears. I flushed, but not with embarrassment.

Mal grinned with pride as I dragged him back up so we were face to face, and kissed him hard. He sighed into it and his hips shifted restlessly against mine, the line of his hard cock burning hot against my hip. The taste of my own release in his mouth and the knowledge that sucking me off had gotten him this worked up was enough to make my dick twitch in interest again—at my age, that was pretty close to a miracle.

"Your turn," I growled into his mouth.

"You don't have to—"

"I want to," I interrupted, and then nipped at his lower lip just to hear him moan.

I could get used to this. I could get used to this really fast.

Chapter 15 - Mal

Priest looked so gorgeous sprawled out on the bed beneath me. His muscled chest, dusted with gray hair, heaved with his exerted breaths, and a flush spread across his cheeks under his neat beard. He looked so relaxed, lax against the sheets, eyes half-closed like he might fall asleep at any moment.

My cock was still throbbing hard, leaking precum where it was pressed against his thigh. It wouldn't take much for me to get off—I was already close to the edge just from the pleasure of getting *him* off. Seeing Priest lose control under my hands and mouth had sent arousal thrumming through me, from the crown of my head all the way to my toes, making me feel hot all over. But there was no urgency to the desire. It just bubbled under the service, warm and pleasurable, and I rocked my hips to press my cock subtly against Priest's hip.

All I needed was a few lazy kisses, and a few dedicated thrusts against the divot of Priest's hip, and the arousal running through me would coil into a warm, rich orgasm. I sprawled half-atop him, mouthing lazy kisses at his neck as I thrust into his hip.

"Hm," Priest said, a low rumble in his chest. "We can't have that."

"What?" I asked, confused, but before I even realized what was happening, Priest swiftly lifted himself up and flipped us, so I was the one on my back with his body half-covering mine. He still looked loose and sated, but the sleepiness had disappeared, replaced by a predatory gleam that sent a shiver down my spine.

"Not gonna let you get off like that," Priest murmured. "Not when I've been dreaming about this for so long."

"Fuck," I said. My toes curled in the sheets as Priest kissed me, then skated one hand down my chest and gripped the base of my cock hard. I gasped as the warm, lazy sense of desire suddenly escalated into a powerful need. His grip wasn't intended to bring me off, though—it was a promise, pulling me back from the edge, but making me want him more.

"So I'm gonna take my time," Priest said in between kisses.

"Hopefully not too long," I muttered.

"I don't think you'll be complaining," Priest teased.

Priest ran his hand up and down my arm as he kissed me, his callused fingers traveling over my shoulder, bicep, across the sensitive skin of my inner elbow, then down to my wrist. My nerves were hypersensitive, his touch sparking across my skin, despite how gentle it was. I let him guide the kiss, and I couldn't do much more than part my lips and let him take what he wanted.

"It's been a long time since I've been with anyone," Priest said again. Then he began to travel down my body, kissing down my chest the same way I'd done to him. He moved his hands, too, restlessly touching whatever skin he could reach. But when I reached for him, he caught my wrists and pressed my hands into the mattress. The subtle show of dominance made my head spin. And I was happy to let him take control. "God, your body is amazing."

My face heated at the praise, but not in a bad way. I squirmed a little under his touch, and Priest immediately grabbed my hips hard, stilling me. Shit. God, it felt good to be pinned like this. It'd been a long time since a man had touched *me* like this, too.

Priest mouthed wet, lingering kisses over my pecs, abs, then down to my hips. My cock throbbed as his lips moved closer to the hard curve of my cock, and it drooled precum onto my belly in anticipation. I curled my hands in the sheets. He was *right there,* his mouth hovering over my cock, close enough that his warm breath washed over my skin, and my abs flexed with the struggle to stay still. All I wanted to do was to thrust up and drive my cock in between his lips.

But he wasn't having it. Instead, he kept moving down. He slid his hands from my hips to my thighs and dug his fingers hard into the muscle. It hurt in the most delicious way, the way a good massage hurts, and I groaned as pleasure ran through me. Priest dropped kisses on my inner thighs, too, kisses with a sharp edge of teeth. I hissed at the pinprick of pain—that only made it feel better. I wondered if it would leave marks. The thought of waking up to mouth-shaped hickeys on my thighs was nearly enough to push me over the edge.

Priest slid off the foot of the bed, then knelt so he could drag his hands over my calves, ankles, ending with kisses right on top of my bare feet. God, it was dizzying, the sheer amount of *attention* he was paying me. Like he wanted to know every inch of my body. I was so fucking turned on—I'd never felt this wound up, this teased.

I was used to being the one in control, and I was used to quick fucks. When I hooked up with guys, it was for one purpose—orgasm. I never fucked like this. Slow, and lazy, and doting. With strangers, I wasn't comfortable feeling this vulnerable. But with Priest, it was natural—and overwhelming. And *so* fucking good.

Then, finally, Priest worked his way back up my body. He crawled back onto the bed and slid his hands up my body from my calves all the way to the curve of my waist, and then he lay down at my side and guided my face to his for another kiss. This time the kiss was deep and messy; Priest seemed just as affected by the slow pace as I was. It was like we were drunk on it, gasping into each other's mouths as our tongues moved languidly.

"Come on," I managed to groan between kisses. "Please."

"Please what?" Priest teased.

"Touch me, you bastard," I said. I was really about to lose it—my cock was throbbing, desperate for sensation. It wasn't going to take much, but I needed Priest's hand on me. And I wasn't too shy to beg. Maybe with someone else I would've been, but not with Priest.

"Since you asked so nicely," Priest said. Then he finally, *finally* touched me where I wanted it most.

He didn't grip the base of my cock hard like he had before. Instead, he pressed the palm of his hand to my cock, pinning my hard length between his palm and my abs. The pressure made my world narrow to that sensation, the buildup making the pleasure nearly overwhelming. I groaned, breaking the kiss to throw my head back against the pillow, and Priest mouthed kisses at my jawline instead.

Priest moved his hand up, over the length of my cock and then the sensitive head, gathering the leaking precum as best he could in his palm. Then he wrapped his hand fully around my cock and slid his hand down slowly.

I groaned his name and wrapped one arm around his shoulders, trying to pull him even closer, while my other hand was still snarled desperately in the sheets. My hips rocked up into his touch, and this time, he didn't pin me down. I planted my feet onto the mattress and thrust into his hand.

"Yeah, like that," Priest growled against my skin, tightening his grip minutely. I was so turned on, cock still drooling precum, making his grip slick and so, so good. I hadn't thought a handjob could *feel* this good.

Then Priest picked up the pace, matching my thrusts. He jerked me off in earnest, and the heat and pleasure that had been swirling inside me since we'd first kissed surged, coiling tight in between my hips.

"Fuck, Priest," I warned. "Gonna come."

"Yeah?" Priest teased, jerking me faster. "Come on, let me see."

Something about knowing he was watching—that he *wanted* to see me—was the last bit I needed to push me over the edge. I moaned, low and loud; my abs tensed, and my heels dug into the mattress as I thrust up into his fist with my head still thrown back. I came harder than I had in years. The sensation coursed over me, crashing like an ocean wave, and I shut my eyes so tightly I saw sparks as I came in ropes over my chest.

I shuddered through it, then collapsed flat onto the mattress, breathing hard as the aftershocks rippled through me.

"Gorgeous," Priest murmured, then kissed me. "Wait here."

"Hm, if you insist," I said, then stretched my arms lazily overhead.

Priest climbed out of bed and padded to the bathroom. I knew I needed to do the same, clean up, but his bed was so comfortable that I was considering falling asleep with cum drying on my chest, regardless of how annoyed I'd be tomorrow.

But then Priest returned a few minutes later, cleaned up with a damp washcloth in hand. He ran it over my chest, carefully cleaning me off, and then tossed the washcloth aside.

"Thanks," I murmured, a little stunned.

I wasn't used to this kind of caretaking. It made me feel a little shy—embarrassed, even—but I liked it, too. Even though it was odd. This was already so different from hookups I'd had in the past. Priest crawled back into bed, scooted close to me, and I stiffened.

He noticed. "Everything okay?"

"Yeah," I said. I took a deep, steadying breath, and intentionally relaxed my muscles, sinking back into the mattress. Priest was on his side next to me, and he rested one hand gently on my chest, rubbing soothing circles there. "Usually at this point, I'd be putting my pants back on and heading out the door," I admitted with a self-deprecating laugh.

"Not a spend-the-night kind of guy, were you?" Priest asked, with a small smile on his face.

"Nah, and the people I hooked up with usually weren't too keen on having me stay, either," I said. "Not like we were trying to form lasting bonds."

"Makes sense," Priest said. "I could go to the couch if you—"

"No," I said immediately, cutting him off. "I want—I want to spend the night with you." It was weird to say it out loud, but it was worth it to see the way Priest relaxed and smiled. "It's just different, you know? Since we know each other so well."

"Yeah," Priest said. "It's a little strange for me, too. But in the opposite way."

"You feel okay about it still?" I asked. I wouldn't be surprised if Priest had changed his mind—if it was *too* strange to be with someone who wasn't Ankh, especially after the first time.

"Yeah, I do. But this is the first time I've been intimate with someone new in over thirty years." He shook his head a little, like he couldn't believe it.

"Hope I wasn't too much of a letdown," I said with a smirk.

"I think you did all right," Priest said. Then he leaned up and kissed me again, and the now-familiar sensation of his lips on mine settled some of my nerves.

"Good," I said. "This was really, really good."

"It was," Priest agreed. "Feels sort of... natural, doesn't it?"

"Yeah," I said. "And I haven't come that hard in a long time."

"Haven't lost my touch, I guess," Priest said with a grin.

We exchanged a few more lazy kisses, and then Priest pulled away. "We'll just take it one day at a time. Does that sound good?"

"As long as we get to do this again, it does," I said.

"Hell, yeah," Priest said, grinning in a way that made him seem younger than he was. "Now get some sleep."

Sleep came surprisingly easy in Priest's big bed, listening to his steady, even breathing. One day at a time.

Chapter 16 - Priest

I woke up to the sun slanting in through the open window of my cabin, as I did every morning. I stretched long in bed, reaching my arms overhead and groaning a little as my shoulders popped. I was always a little stiff and slow-moving when I first woke up, and I shifted a little on the mattress, stretching through my lats to relieve some of the tension there.

Next to me, Mal sighed in his sleep and pulled the blanket a little tighter around himself.

I stilled as the events of last night came rushing back. I stopped stretching and then slowly slid out of bed, careful not to disturb Mal. I finished my stretch while standing instead, feeling my spine lengthen and pop as I gazed down at the shape of Mal under the covers.

He murmured and rolled over, so he was facing me, but he was still fast asleep. The covers were snug around his shoulders, and his lips were slightly parted, his face soft and younger-looking in sleep. An odd, protective urge made my heart clench in my chest. I was so used to seeing Mal in president-mode—not like this. Finally at ease. And I liked being the one to make him feel that way, at least in small part. He spent so much time leading the club, keeping us all together and safe... He deserved a safe place to put some of that responsibility down.

And if that place was our friendship, then that was even better. Deep inside, though, I wondered if that was sustainable. If that wouldn't push our friendship into something more. Something that he wasn't ready for, and I wasn't sure if I was, either.

Couldn't deny the fact that he was so gorgeous, though—and the sex *had* been great. I felt better rested than I had in years, too; I'd always slept better with someone beside me. And the incredible orgasms didn't hurt, either. I pulled on a sweatshirt then slipped into the bathroom to brush my teeth. In the mirror, I even *looked* more rested, with a youthful glimmer in my eyes. I'd gotten so used to seeing my face looking a little dull and exhausted lately. I'd forgotten I could look like this.

I looked happy.

I grimaced around my toothbrush and looked down into the sink instead. Did it really take so little for me to feel happy again? I couldn't help the guilt that cut through me, cold and sudden at the idea. But, I reminded myself, it was like Mal had said last night. He wasn't trying to replace Ankh, and neither was I.

It was just sex. Sex with someone I trusted and respected. And from the way I looked and felt this morning, it was clear the experience was good for me. Besides, just because we'd had sex didn't mean we were falling in love—we'd established that clearly between us. One day at a time. I didn't need to feel like I was betraying Ankh, because I *wasn't*. This was just another way for me to heal, and to lean on Mal as a friend.

That was all I needed right now, at my age, with the grief of losing Ankh still weighing on me. A good friend, a little something more.

The guilt melted away as I finished brushing my teeth, and I even let a smile play on my lips. It felt good to feel good. I wasn't going to let this nugget of happiness slip away.

I snuck down the stairs, moving quietly so as to not wake Mal, and put the coffee on. I puttered around the living room as I usually did in the mornings, taking time sipping my coffee and enjoying the quiet stillness of the morning. About a half-hour later, Mal stumbled down the stairs, rubbing his eyes and grimacing at the bright light in the kitchen.

"Coffee," he demanded in a grumble still scratchy with sleep.

I chuckled to myself, leaning against the counter with my second cup of coffee in my hand. "Not much of a morning person, huh?"

"Ugh," he said. "Coffee, please."

I pointed to the cabinet, and Mal clumsily procured himself a mug and poured the coffee in. He sighed with relief as he took his first sip, eyes fluttering closed like it was the most delicious thing he'd ever tasted. For all the years I'd known Mal, I'd never seen him like this. He was funny in the morning, moving sleepily and grumpily around the kitchen. It was intimate. Familiar. Like this was part of our everyday routine.

It made me smile to start my day with someone else again, to wake up together and share coffee and idle conversation—and I liked seeing Mal this way, soft and moody, before he shifted into president mode in the clubhouse.

Even though I loved the cabin the guys had built for me, I hadn't been able to shake the feeling that it'd been missing something. I realized, as I watched Mal peer into the fridge and squawk with indignity that I only had *nonfat* yogurt, that it wasn't some*thing* missing. It was some*one*.

The cabin was gorgeous, and well-made, and comfortable... and when it was just me, it was *lonely*. Having Mal here went a long way toward filling that gap I hadn't been able to place. I'd been longing to have another heartbeat in my space.

"This shit is bad for you," Mal said, brandishing my fruit-at-the-bottom nonfat yogurt. "It's all sugar. Just get the full-fat stuff and put in fresh fruit."

"All right, I will next time," I said with a grin. "You're still going to eat it, though, aren't you?"

"Hell, yeah, I am," Mal said, peeling the lid off the yogurt container. "It's delicious."

I laughed, shaking my head fondly. "I'm gonna get dressed and then head over to the clubhouse. You coming with?"

"Yeah, definitely," Mal said. "I'm almost awake. This coffee is good."

"Only the finest," I said. "And I did splurge for a coffeemaker slightly nicer than the one in the clubhouse."

"Priorities," Mal agreed.

"How are you feeling?" I asked. "Sleep all right?"

"Slept really well," Mal said. "Better than I have in a while." He paused and set his yogurt and coffee aside. He tilted his head, watching me curiously. "What about you?"

"About the same. I finally feel like I got some *real* sleep."

I turned back to the coffeemaker to refill my mug, just another half-cup of coffee to sip on while we walked to the clubhouse. Then, I made a small sound of surprise as Mal's arms wound around my waist from behind. He set his chest flush to my back, hooking his chin over my shoulder.

"Good," he said. "I think this was a good development. What are you thinking?"

I smiled, then knocked my temple gently against his. "I think so, too. It's nice, waking up like this. With you."

"Agreed," Mal said. "We should do it again sometime."

I laughed as he pressed a chaste, almost playful kiss to my neck before pulling away. "And hey," I said.

Mal raised his eyebrows curiously as he picked his yogurt back up.

"Thanks for—being so communicative," I said. "Makes this a lot easier."

Mal just smiled and nodded, like it wasn't a big deal at all. But it was to me. To have this kind of closeness with someone I trusted, and who understood and respected my boundaries and my confusions around Ankh—I didn't know how to tell him how grateful I was.

That'd have to come later. Right now, we had to go back to the clubhouse and start handling this Xavier situation. That took precedence over hashing out the details of this development with Mal. We both got dressed, shrugged on our respective leather jackets, and then walked the short distance from my cabin to the clubhouse. Even the silence between us was good.

The clubhouse was bustling with activity despite the fairly early hour. Rebel, Coop, Gunnar, Raven, and Dante were at the kitchen island, Blade was making another pot of coffee, and Logan was perched on the kitchen counter with a croissant in his hand.

"Hey, guys," Mal called as he stepped inside. "Morning."

"Morning," everyone answered in unison.

"Everything okay last night?" I asked. "Anything fishy?"

"Not a thing," Raven said. "Nothing out of place at the motel, either, according to Star and Eli. They stopped in earlier today."

"Good," I said. "Any other updates?"

"Xavier was questioned by the police last night," Rebel said. "I got the update this morning. He denied everything, obviously, and he has an alibi for the suspected time window of the break-in, verified by his colleagues at work."

"Fuck," Mal said. "What's that mean for us?"

"The police are going to come gather evidence today, as a favor to me," Rebel said, "but they're not going to run any DNA tests on our gut feeling alone. We need something more substantial. Right now, it just looks like things are missing—we don't have much that makes it seem like a *break-in* at all."

"But it *is*," Blade growled. "We all know that."

"Yeah, we know that," Logan agreed. "But we can't get the cops to just *believe* us. They need something concrete."

I cringed and rubbed my forehead, exasperated. This wasn't the news I wanted to hear—I'd been hoping they'd bag Xavier with no problems. But if he'd been able to get into the motel undetected, he obviously knew what he was doing. *Of course* he had an alibi. He probably had his next attack already planned.

"We obviously haven't heard the last of this guy," I said. "Until he's in custody with the cops, we're not taking any chances with Mal's—or anyone's—safety."

"I agree," Blade said, and then gave me a curious look. I flushed slightly. Rarely did I make outbursts like that—with slightly more temper than the guys were used to hearing from me. "If anything, we're going to tighten security even more."

Mal nodded gratefully. I stepped a little closer to him, almost unconsciously, and set my hand at his lower back. He relaxed a little under the touch, and shot me a smile— soft, small, and private. A smile I was getting really addicted to seeing.

Then he bit his lower lip and nodded toward the kitchen island, where all the guys were sitting silently, staring at us. I dropped my hand but didn't step away from Mal; clearly that touch was a little more intimate than the guys were used to seeing from us. But at the same time, I didn't want to hide, either.

Gunnar raised his eyebrows and elbowed Raven. "Dude, your dad is banging the president."

"Gunnar!" Raven squawked. "Dante, admonish him!"

Dante tilted his head to the side a little, and I recognized Mal in the gesture, which made me smile a little. "I don't know," Dante said. "Gunnar might be onto something."

"Guys, guys," Mal said, raising his hands before the room could devolve into chaos. "Let's get one thing clear. We didn't *bang*." He caught my eye and winked at me.

"Right," I said, grinning as I realized what he was getting at. "Of course we didn't bang. Maybe there were some wandering hands—"

"—wandering mouths, too," Mal noted.

"And maybe we kept each other up pretty late."

"Way too late," Mal said. "So first, what happened—"

"No, no, no, no, no!" Dante plugged his ears. "I'm good, I'm good!"

Raven did the same, clapping his hands over his ears and shrieking his refusal of details, but he was beaming at the same time.

"I knew it!" Gunnar said, standing up. "Blade, pay up!"

"We didn't bet anything!" Blade said.

The room dissolved into laughter, and then Joker came thumping down the stairs half-dressed and rolling his eyes. "What the hell is going on down here?" he asked. "I'm not supposed to be awake for, like, two more hours!"

That just made everyone laugh harder. I swung my arm around Mal's shoulder and tugged him close to my side, just because I could. From where he was seated at the kitchen island, Raven caught my eye. A huge grin spread across his face, and he nodded, his blue eyes glittering with happiness as he watched Mal and me.

I hadn't been worried about it, but I was still relieved to see all the guys take this change in our relationship in stride. No one even seemed shocked, honestly. I assumed they understood this the same way that I did—that it was a natural extension of our decades of friendship, at a time when we both needed a little extra support.

Mal wrapped his arm around my waist, under my jacket so he could press his fingers possessively into the curve of my waist. Whatever was going with Xavier, we'd get it all under control. I'd take care of the club—I'd take care of Mal. It was what I did best, and I wasn't going to let him down now.

Chapter 17 - Mal

It'd been a couple of weeks since the break-in at the motel, and I still hadn't heard anything from Xavier. The silence made me nervous, but it wasn't keeping me up at night. And good thing, too, especially on early mornings like this, when Dante needed an extra hand at the bakery.

I rolled the bagel dough into a cylinder, then curled it around my knuckles to form the ring shape, before rolling it again on the workbench to seal the edges together. I set it aside and repeated the process with another, and another—these were the kinds of tasks Dante called me in to help with, tedious tasks for unexpected big orders. Someone had to shape these fifty bagels, and Dante certainly didn't have time to do it. He was across from me, working on shaping the sourdough loaves for tomorrow.

"How are things at the motel?" Dante asked. "Anyone report any problems with the upgrades?"

"No complaints at all," I said. "For such a quick turnaround, they really did a good job."

"Benefits of having an in with the construction guys," Dante said with a grin.

Raven, Brennan, and Dawson had worked together to get the security upgraded quickly, with cameras and alarms, and they even replaced all the windows with new ones, with heavier-duty locks.

"Gotta say," he said, "I was pretty surprised you moved back in right when the construction was finished."

"Why wouldn't I?" I asked with faux ignorance. "I missed my apartment."

And that was true. I *had* missed my apartment and waking up to the chaos of the members in the motel. But at the same time...

"No reason," Dante said with a shrug. "Only that you seemed pretty comfortable crashing with Priest. I thought you might ride that wave a little longer."

"Didn't want to overstay my welcome," I said simply. "He got that cabin for a reason. He deserves a little privacy."

"Hm," Dante said, clearly not buying it. "How are things with you two?"

I turned my attention to the bagels I was shaping, mostly to avoid meeting Dante's gaze as I pondered that question.

"They're good," I said, before I could think too hard. "Really good." I glanced up. "Not sure how much detail you're looking for here, son."

It was true, though. Things *were* going well. I'd spent every night during the motel construction in Priest's bed, but we hadn't fooled around every night. And that's what we'd been doing—fooling around. We hadn't had full-on sex yet, and neither of seemed to be in a hurry to do so. It was nice just to have someone to hold close at night, and kiss in the morning.

And that was one of the reasons I'd been eager to move back into the motel as soon as I could. Priest had said I was welcome as long as I wanted to stay with him, if I didn't feel safe in the motel—and part of me had considered staying longer, just because I could. And that was dangerous. It was dangerously easy to fold Priest into my life—to get used to sleeping in his bed and sharing lazy kisses over coffee in the kitchen.

Every time something like that happened—something familiar and domestic—I remembered what we'd discussed before we got involved with his. We were friends first, and not fucking up this friendship was my top priority. I didn't want to get too emotionally entangled. Priest was still grieving Ankh, and the worst thing I could do was start wanting something he wasn't prepared to give me. I'd been abandoned once before, and I didn't want to go through that pain again. It was better for us both if I put a little distance between us, so we could keep taking care of each other without getting overly close.

"You know me and the guys are just teasing when we say we don't want to hear it," Dante said. "You can talk to me about anything—including Priest."

"Well," I said, still focused on the bagels, "we're just friends with benefits. That's working really well for us. We both like to have our own space, so of course once the motel was ready, I moved back in."

My phone buzzed and pinged in my pocket, and I hurriedly wiped the flour onto the apron I was wearing before fishing it out of my pocket.

"Right," Dante said, sounding unconvinced. "For a man who likes his space, you sure do go for that phone fast."

I rolled my eyes. "I'm simply trying to stay on top of club business."

"Sure," Dante said, then laughed and went back to shaping his loaves.

I opened the message.

It was from an unknown number. My heart immediately sank, and my stomach twisted with nerves.

"How could you do this to us?" it read. *"I know we have something special. I miss you."*

"What is it?" Dante asked, looking suddenly concerned. "You don't look so good."

I sighed and walked around the bench to show Dante the message. His face immediately fell. "It's him, isn't it?"

"Yeah," I said. "Xavier. I assume it's about the DNA results."

After the cops had initially refused to run DNA testing, we'd pushed back with the restraining order as well as a detailed record of all the stalking and threats. It'd been embarrassing to reveal to the police the details of my sex life, but it'd worked. I didn't know if the police had found anything, but they must be contacting Xavier again if he was texting me sounding so betrayed. I took my phone back from Dante and blocked the number with a sigh.

"That guy is a fucking psycho," Dante said, sneering. "Don't worry about it. We're closing in on him—it'll be over soon."

"Yeah, I know it'll be fine," I said with a sigh. "I'm just getting pretty sick of it."

And it wasn't who I'd wanted to hear from. It was ridiculous—but now that I wasn't staying at the cabin, I *missed* Priest. I craved his presence constantly. And that was a sign that I'd done the right thing in backing off.

"Hey, guys." That warm familiar voice made me spin on my heel toward the open doorframe to the bakery's front room, and suddenly all thoughts of distance fled. Priest was behind the counter as Mary dealt with the customers, leaning on the doorframe like he wasn't sure if he was allowed into the kitchen. "Am I interrupting?"

"No, your timing is great," Dante said with a grin. "I can finish up here, Dad. Thanks for the help."

I stepped out of the kitchen into the busy bakery. It was mid-morning, and the communal tables were dotted with people enjoying coffee and pastries, and a regular stream of community members came in and out, grabbing things to-go. Priest already had two coffees waiting for us.

"What's going on?" I asked, smiling as he led me outside to one of the small tables on the sidewalk. "Need to talk about something?"

"No, no," Priest said. "I just had some time to kill before I show the prospects some new things at Ankhor Works, and word was you were at Stella's this morning, so I thought I'd swing by."

We sat down at the small table, close enough that our feet knocked together under it. God, it was good to see him especially after the whiplash of receiving that text after so many weeks of radio silence. I sighed and wrapped my hands around the mug of coffee.

"Good timing," I said.

"What do you mean?" Priest asked. "What happened?"

I pulled up the text again and handed my phone to him.

He read it, then grimaced. "So he's back to texting you?"

"This is the first one I've gotten since the break-in. I'm assuming the cops are questioning him again."

"There's not going to be anything left of him to question if he starts pulling this shit again," Priest said in a low growl. "I know we agreed to wait on club justice, but I'm starting to change my mind."

"It's just a text," I said, then hooked my foot around his ankle. "If anything, the cops getting under his skin is a good thing."

"Can't say I agree," Priest said. "I think this guy is long overdue for an ass kicking."

Seeing Priest get all huffy and protective of me because of a nasty text did, in a funny way, lift my mood. It made me feel cared for, in a way I hadn't in a long, long time. Typically, *I* was the one doing the protecting and the threatening, and being on the opposite end of that felt strangely good.

"I know, I'm sick of it, too. I can't believe how long this has dragged out. If I had known a stupid hookup could go this badly, I never would've started going out to Stallions at all. Ain't worth the trouble, that's for sure."

"I can't believe I didn't even know you were hanging out at Stallions," Priest said. "Why were you keeping it a secret? I'm sure you could've wrangled some of the younger guys to go with you, make a whole production of it."

I sighed and rubbed the back of my neck. "It's not something I was exactly proud of," I said. "I wasn't going to have a good time, to make a night of it. I really was just looking to hook up."

"So what?" Priest asked. "*That's* a good time."

I grinned. "Yeah, I guess you're right. Don't really need to worry about that anymore, though—I don't think I'll be going to Stallions anytime soon."

Priest raised his eyebrows at me meaningfully, and I laughed and knocked my foot against his again.

"And what's so wrong with having a few secrets?" I asked. "I thought it was harmless, and I didn't really want to go out hunting with club members, either. It was nice to have some alone time."

He nodded. "Yeah, I understand that. If you go out with club members, you still have to be their president."

"Exactly," I said. Priest just *understood.* "And I'm sure you have secrets, too."

Priest shrugged. "Not really. I'm an open book."

I rolled my eyes. "That's *not* true."

"What? It is!"

"Maybe you're an open book, but you spend so much time worrying about everyone else that you don't actually *talk* about yourself," I said, then peered knowingly over my coffee at him.

Priest shrugged a little, then rubbed his hand over his hair, but he didn't deny it. "Well. What do you want to know?"

I didn't have any particular burning questions, but there was a gap in my knowledge that suddenly jumped to my mind. "You know, we met when you and Ankh moved here to start Hell's Ankhor."

"Right," Priest said.

"I don't know your wallet name," I said—meaning the legal name on his ID card. "Never had to bail you out of jail or anything."

Priest barked a laugh, sudden and surprised. "Are you serious?"

"As a heart attack!" I insisted. "It's never come up. Not like it's important."

"Wow," Priest said. "Thirty years and it's never come up." He shook his head in disbelief. "It's Harry. Well, Harold, technically, but I always went by Harry before I got my tag."

Harry. I peered thoughtfully at him. "Hm. It's a nice name, but I think I'm going to stick with Priest."

"Please do," he said through his laughter. "It'd be too weird if you suddenly started calling me Harry. Ankh didn't even do that, unless he was mad at me or trying to make up for something." He laughed again, and it was tinged with wistfulness. "He really could have a temper when he was younger. Volatile moods. It was one of the things that drew me to him."

He sighed, and his gaze was slightly unfocused as he got caught up in the memory. I waited patiently, sipping my coffee. Priest didn't continue, though, he just shook himself like he hadn't meant to go silent.

"Sorry," he said, flushing a little. "I don't mean to spend all this time talking about Ankh."

"What?" I asked. I tilted my head, genuinely surprised. "You don't need to apologize for talking about him. I'd like to hear what you were thinking about—if you want to share."

Priest's gaze softened.

"He was my friend, too," I said. "I don't want you to think you shouldn't talk about him. Especially between the two of us—I know it's different to talk about him with someone who knew him as a friend and not just the president."

"You're right," Priest said. "It really is different. Thank you." He got that wistful look again, a small smile playing at the corners of his lips. "He was really cute and naïve when we first met. We'd hooked up at a bar, made out, all of that—and then he reveals to me he was straight. Apparently, I'd turned his world upside down."

"Doesn't surprise me," I said with a grin. "I've seen pictures of you from those years."

"Oh, lay off," Priest said, but he was still smiling. "We got closer, kept going on dates, and I knew he was still feeling a little scared about the connection between us, but I thought I'd take it one day at a time. So when he disappeared one day, I figured that was the end of it. I was pretty heartbroken, but I knew the risks of getting involved with a 'straight' guy, so I tried to move on. Couldn't, obviously. And then a few weeks later, he showed up at my door super apologetic, with flowers and this big new plan to start a *club* with me."

He laughed, shaking his head. "That man. He always had these big ideas. I almost turned him away when he showed up like that, but he was so passionate, I decided to give it another shot."

"Glad you did," I said. "Or else I would've been picking up the pieces."

Priest started. "What do you mean?"

"He never told you?" I asked, eyes widening.

"Told me what?" Priest asked.

"About those weeks apart?"

"No!" Priest said. "I figured it was private. Getting his thoughts straightened out. Or less straightened out, I guess, forgive the pun."

"Awful. Terrible pun." I shook my head. "And you never asked?"

"It didn't seem important," Priest said with a shrug. "All I cared about was that he'd decided to come back. Why? Did he talk to you about it?"

I could hardly believe it. All that time together and Ankh had never mentioned what he'd been doing those weeks.

"He came back to our hometown," I said. "He wanted to talk to the only out gay guy he knew."

Priest's eyes widened.

"Yeah. Me."

"No way." Priest slapped the table and laughed in pure disbelief. "He didn't!"

"He absolutely did," I said with a grin. "Aaron showed up at my doorstep freaking out with this long story about this guy he'd met at a bar, and how he'd never felt anything like this for anyone before."

Priest looked absolutely floored. The memory made me smile, too—I could see it clear as day in my mind, Ankh's windswept dark hair and his brow furrowed above his deep blue eyes, talking a mile a minute as he often did when he got anxious. I'd had to interrupt him to get him to slow down and encourage him to come into the Liberty Crew clubhouse for a beer and the chance to actually explain what was going on.

At the time I'd been afraid it was something awful—when he'd explained that it was just guy problems, and not even real *problems* at that, I'd laughed so hard I'd almost cried, much to Aaron's chagrin.

"I was already in the Liberty Crew at the time," I said. "So he crashed at the clubhouse for a while and nearly drove himself insane thinking in circles."

"That law school brain of his," Priest said. "Always had to look at every problem from every angle."

"Exactly," I said with a smile. "I told him there wasn't anything to be afraid of. He should just follow his heart. He didn't seem to believe me, until one day he woke up and said I was right."

"Always had to come to the conclusions on his own, too," Priest said. "God, that drove me crazy. So, it was staying at the Crew Motel that gave him the idea to start the club, huh?"

"Well," I said, and bit my lip a little sheepishly, "I may have had something to do with that, too."

"What!" Priest squawked. He threw his hands up, rocking back in his chair so hard that it rattled the table. "How is it possible that I didn't know this?"

"I didn't *tell* him to start the club," I said, laughing as I picked up my coffee mug to keep it from sloshing on the table. "I may have planted the seed of the idea, but the execution was all him."

"What did you do?" Priest asked.

"He just seemed really lost," I said with a shrug. "Falling in love with you kind of threw a wrench in all his plans. He was always a guy who liked to build things, you know. Communities, and businesses, and all that. But that rebellious streak was always getting him into trouble."

"Never *stopped* getting him into trouble," Priest agreed.

"He was a born leader, as you know," I said, and Priest nodded. "So, I knew he wouldn't really be interested in the idea of prospecting. But the idea of building something—I thought it might be a good next step for him. And a way for him to show in a concrete way that he was committed to you." I rubbed my chin, still smiling at the memory. "I told him if I was in your position, I'd be really fucking pissed that the guy I was into just ran out on me like that."

"I *was* pissed," Priest said. "And you were right. When he proposed the idea of starting a club together, I knew he was serious."

"What can I say?" I asked. "I'm a romantic."

"Wow," Priest said, "So really we have *you* to thank for Hell's Ankhor, don't we?"

"Hell, no," I said. "All I did was give him a push. Building it was all you two."

Priest took a sip of his coffee, still grinning like he couldn't control it. I realized suddenly that I hadn't seen him in smile like that in... well, in years. Not since he lost Ankh. And sitting here over coffee, reminiscing about our shared connections with Ankh, was the happiest I'd felt in a long time, too.

Chapter 18 - Priest

"Wow," I said again, still reeling from the story Mal had just shared with me. "I can't believe this. If it weren't for you, Ankh and I may not have had the life we did together."

Mal just smiled. "Nah, you would've figured things out regardless. I'm glad I got to help speed things up, though."

It was just like Ankh—still leaving me things to discover about him even after he was gone.

"Maybe so," I said. "But I'm glad we got to be each other's first."

"First what?" Mal asked, eyebrows raised.

"What? What do you mean?" I asked, raising my eyebrows right back.

"Not his first kiss," Mal said.

"First with a man, yeah," I said. Ankh had been straight before me. We hadn't ever discussed the specifics of that, but I'd just assumed...

"Well," Mal said. "Gotta say I beat you to it."

"What!" I said again, and I was so shocked I stood up fast enough to rattle the table again. I started laughing incredulously, overwhelmed by surprise and joy and humor. "You're fucking kidding me! You didn't!"

"We were teenagers!" Mal shouted, laughing too, his coffee held protectively in his hand. Inside the bakery, customers were starting to shoot us dirty looks for how disruptive we were being, audible even through the glass of the front window.

I gathered myself and sat back down at the table with a pointed sigh. "So what you're saying is…"

"I came out as bisexual pretty young. And when we were teenagers, Aaron was starting to feel curious, too. So he asked me how I knew, and we got to talking—there may have been some stolen booze involved—and I offered to kiss him to see if he liked it. So we kissed, and it was fine, but there wasn't any real spark there." Mal smiled at the memory. "He thought that meant he was straight. Turns out it just meant that he and I didn't have any real chemistry. We were always supposed to be friends."

I shook my head. This was a lot of new information about Ankh to absorb, and it thrilled me. It made me feel closer to Ankh's memory—and closer to Mal, as well. We'd always been good friends, but these past few weeks had made our friendship even stronger.

And… sometimes it felt like more than a friendship. Even when we weren't in bed together.

Mal threw his head back and laughed. He was so handsome like this, open and expressive, and I loved spending time with him. Now more than ever. It was just how I was wired—I always preferred relationships to casual arrangements… and nothing about my friendship with Mal was casual. I'd thought that I'd never be able to offer another man the kind of commitment a long-term relationship deserved. But the more time I spent with Mal, the more I thought it might be possible. Possible because Mal loved Ankh just as much as I had, albeit in a different way.

"Hope that doesn't bother you," Mal said. His tone was teasing, but I could tell from his expression he was a little nervous.

"Bother's not exactly the right word," I said, low. There was a meaningful cyclicality to it all—that Mal and Ankh had their youthful exploratory experiences, then Ankh and I were together in such a defining way, and now Mal and I had found our way to each other.

"Oh?" Mal asked, the nerves replaced with a curious heat in his eyes.

Screw the people inside. Screw causing a scene. I leaned over the table, took Mal's coffee out of his hand, then tugged him toward me with my hand fisted in the front of his shirt. I kissed him hard, passionately, desire thrumming through my body as his tongue slipped into my mouth.

"Hey," I murmured against his lips.

Inside the bakery, someone whistled.

"Hey," Mal said, sounding just as turned on as I felt.

"Wanna get out of here?" I asked.

"Is that why you showed up to bother me at work?" Mal teased. "Trying to get laid?"

"Nah, I just like hanging out with you," I said. "But something about you *does* get me going."

We shared one more burning kiss before we both hopped on our bikes and rode the short distance to the motel. Riding alongside Mal on the two-lane highway only heightened my anticipation. Something about the thrumming of my engine beneath me, and the knowledge that the man controlling that beast of a bike beside me would be under me (or above me?) in just a few minutes made my pulse ratchet up.

We parked outside the motel, and Siren and Coop, our enforcement detail, were not far behind us. I tugged off my helmet and shot them a grin over my shoulder.

"Y'all might want to hang out outside for a while," I said, the implication dripping from my words like honey.

"Gross," Coop said. "How long is a while?"

"We're gonna find out," Mal growled, and tugged me over the threshold into the lobby of the motel.

Luckily, it was quiet in the motel. I chased Mal up the stairs to his studio apartment, smacking his ass playfully as he went ahead of me. "You better watch it," he growled over his shoulder.

"Or what?" I teased as desire shot through me. "What are you going to do about it?"

We made it into the hall just outside his door, and Mal grabbed me by the lapels of my jacket and slammed me hard against the wall. The club photos hanging rattled with the force of it, and my breath expelled from my lungs in a surprised huff. Mal's dark eyes bore into mine as he drew his lower lip between his teeth.

I used the moment of stillness to use the same move on him, flipping us suddenly so Mal was the one against the wall. He laughed incredulously as I did so, then tipped his head back against the wall and looked down the bridge of his nose at me, like he was taunting me.

I growled with desire, then boxed him in against the wall further and dragged my teeth over the skin of his neck. God, I wanted him—wanted to *fuck* him, with an intensity that surprised me. I wanted to pin his strong body beneath mine and make him cry out my name.

"Nice move," Mal groaned. He wriggled a hand between us and palmed my cock hard through my jeans, then gripped it almost hard enough to hurt.

I gasped—but if he'd thought that little trick would give him the upper hand, he was wrong. I just pushed closer, wrenched his jacket and the collar of his shirt aside to reveal his shoulder, and then I bit down *hard.* Enough that there'd be a bruise tomorrow.

"Fucking hell," Mal gasped. For a second I thought I'd gone too far, but then he muttered, *"Priest,"* sounding more wrecked than I'd ever heard him. I swatted his hand away from my dick, and he stared at me again, pupils dilated and lower lip swollen from where he'd sank his teeth.

The sight was intoxicating. "Come on," I growled, then grabbed him by the front of the shirt and hauled him into his bedroom.

*

MAL

Priest maneuvered me into my apartment, walking me backward with his hands on my hips and a sexy, promising smirk on his face. He tossed me bodily back onto the mattress, and I landed with a whump in the center of my bed, still reeling from the rough way he'd handled me in the hallway. My skin tingled where he'd sunk his teeth into my shoulder, so possessive and demanding. It thrilled me—made me want to roll over for him, but at the same time, I wanted to fight back. Wanted to see him playfully use the strength in his sturdy chest and thick arms to control me.

With a wicked grin, Priest shrugged out of his jacket and then crawled over me on the bed. He kissed me hard, demandingly, fucking his tongue into my mouth and making me gasp.

He started to work a hand up my shirt, and I used the moment of distraction to hook my leg under his and flip us both. Those self-defense lessons Dante and Jazz made us all take were finally paying off. Priest laughed, surprised as he landed on his back. I straddled his hips and shrugged off my jacket, then roughly ripped my shirt over my head. I wanted his skin on mine, and I wanted it *now*.

Priest hummed appreciatively and ran his hands over my abs, then up to my waist and gripped hard, his fingers digging into the muscle there. I wriggled against him, pressing my ass into the curve of his cock trapped in his jeans. He'd already been so hard when I'd grabbed him in the hallway, and I wanted to feel it inside me.

"You're so fucking sexy," Priest groaned, and then slid one hand up my back to my nape. He gripped the back of my neck hard and used that grip to pull me down for another rough kiss. It knocked me off balance a little, and he used that to his advantage, rolling us yet again.

God, I loved this this part. I loved a little rough, wrestling foreplay—loved being with a man who could match my strength, who I didn't have to worry about hurting. When I was hooking up with strangers, I usually didn't go for guys that looked like they could toss me around—simply because I didn't let just anyone do that. But when Priest manhandled me like this, it made me burn hot with desire. Because I trusted him—I knew he'd give me what I wanted, make it last and make it *good*, and I was more than willing to give up control to him.

I wasn't just willing—I *wanted* to. I wanted to so fucking badly.

Priest popped the button on my jeans and wrenched them off me, then tossed them aside unceremoniously so I was in just my tight boxer-briefs. His rich blue gaze traveled over my body hungrily. I wasn't sure what I expected him to do—but it wasn't this.

He flipped me over, easy as anything, so I was flat on my belly on the bed. He gathered both of my wrists in one hand and pinned them over my head. I gasped at the sensation—with his hand on my wrists, and his hips straddling mine, I was completely at his mercy. I shifted beneath him, tried to move my wrists, and I couldn't.

I was pinned.

Something inside me released, and I shivered and sank deeply into the mattress, prone beneath him. Priest hummed again in approval, then leaned down and kissed my jaw, my neck, my shoulder.

"Gorgeous," he said, in a voice so low it was nearly inaudible. "Look at you."

"Fuck, that feels good," I murmured.

Priest ran his free hand down my side to my hip. He tucked his fingers into the waistband of my boxer-briefs, and then snapped the elastic hard against my skin. I gasped at the sensation, squirmed, but I couldn't move with the way Priest was still straddling me.

"Couldn't stop thinking about you like this," Priest admitted. He circled his palm on my hip where he'd snapped the waistband, soothing the sting.

"Like how?" I encouraged. "Tell me."

"Thought about that huge fucking dildo you have," Priest admitted. He snapped the elastic again, and I gasped. The edge of pain was so good, only heightening my anticipation.

"What was I doing with it?" I asked breathlessly. God, I'd been so embarrassed when he'd seen it, and the thought that he imagined me using it sent a thrill up my spine. A blend of shame and arousal raced through me—and the shame made the desire a little hotter. An unexpected but intoxicating blend.

"Want to see you fuck yourself with it," Priest said. Then he brought his hand down on my ass, over my boxer-briefs—not hard enough to really hurt, but enough to make a sound. I gasped again and pressed my face into the pillow like I wanted to hide. God, it was so fucking good. "Work that toy into you while I blow you," Priest continued. "Really make you lose your mind."

"Oh, Christ," I groaned. "Yeah, I want that."

"Not this time, though," Priest said, and spanked me again. "This time I want to fuck you."

He released my wrists finally, but I kept them where they were. Priest was still straddling my thighs, just under my ass, and he kneaded my cheeks with both hands roughly.

"Fuck, yeah," I groaned. "Yeah, come on, I want that, Priest, please."

"God, I love it when you say please," Priest said, low.

He shifted off my thighs and then grabbed my hips, hiking me up onto my knees, so I was propped on the mattress on my knees and elbows. The bed shifted and he disappeared for a moment—I kept my eyes closed, flushed with a blend of arousal and embarrassment at being arranged like this and then abandoned. Just waiting for him to come back and fuck me.

I heard him shucking off his jeans, and then rifling through my nightstand—he knew what I had in there. Fuck, that made me hot, too.

Then he was behind me, smoothing one hand down over my back. He wound that same arm around my waist and slid his hand down to grip my cock.

I cried out his name at the touch—the rough edge to it made my hips jerk and pulse. I was so fucking hard—I'd been hard since he'd pinned me to the wall. He gave me a few slow, dirty strokes, and my thighs quaked. I felt like I wasn't even going to be able to hold myself up for long, I was already so overwhelmed.

"God, you have a perfect ass," Priest murmured. He let go of my cock, and it hung hard and heavy, dripping precum onto the sheets beneath me. He kneaded my ass with both hands again, spreading me. The pressure of his fingers in the muscle of my ass was so good, I couldn't help but arch my back a little, wanting more. Wanting him inside me, *now*.

"Fuck," Priest said in a tone that sounded a little awed. "Yeah, I'm gonna take care of you."

"Get a fucking move on, then," I said, and my voice was rough with desire.

Priest laughed, surprised, and smacked my ass fondly. "Demanding."

I was about to say something snarky back, but then there was the familiar click of the lube opening, and Priest's slick fingers running down my ass crack and over my hole. He circled his touch over my hole teasingly for a moment, but thankfully, he was as eager as I was. He folded his body over mine, holding himself up with one arm while he drove two fingers inside me.

I inhaled sharply at the sudden intrusion. It'd been a while since I'd been on the bottom, and I knew I was tight. Priest made that clear, too, with the way he groaned into the back of my neck as I clenched around his fingers. I exhaled long and slow, purposefully relaxing, and then Priest began to slowly thrust his fingers in and out. Fuck, it felt good— I'd almost forgotten *how* good, until he curled his fingers just so and sent pleasure racing up my spine.

I gasped as he hit that spot inside me again and again, and it only got better when he slid a third finger in, the stretch and the pressure driving all coherent thought from my mind.

"That's enough," I managed to say when he twisted his wrist, fucking three fingers easily into me. "Come on, Priest, *fuck* me."

"That what you want?" Priest asked. He slowed down his pace, fucking me slowly but thoroughly with his hand.

"Yeah," I gasped. I knew what he wanted, that little shit. "Yeah, Priest, *please.*"

"Fuck, Mal," Priest said. He withdrew his fingers. I peered over my shoulder, best I could on elbows and knees. Saliva gathered under my tongue at the sight of Priest rolling on a condom and jerking his huge cock a few times. He caught me looking and smirked. Fuck, I was really in for a ride.

He gripped my hips and slid his cock between my ass cheeks—not inside me, just in between, and then fucked in between like that, a slick drag that had the head of his cock catching on my hole. He groaned, squeezing my ass cheeks together. He threw his head back, sweat beading at the hollow of his throat.

"Fuck, Mal, I'm not gonna last long."

"Then get on with it," I said, pushing my hips back insistently.

Then, finally, Priest got into position. The head of his cock nudged against my hole and he gasped. Then, slowly, he pushed inside.

Fuck, it felt incredible. Huge. Hot. Just on the edge of too much. Priest pressed slowly, slowly inside me until he was finally sheathed all the way, his hips flush against my ass. He held himself up with his hands on either side of me, his chest to my back as he mouthed sloppy kisses on my neck and shoulder. I was surrounded by him on all sides. God, his cock was huge—and I wanted more.

"Fuck me," I said, shifting my hips demandingly against him.

"Gonna," Priest groaned. "Trying not to blow my load immediately. You're so fucking *tight.*"

Then Priest shifted his weight to one hand so he could grip my cock with the other. I moaned, toes curling as intense pleasure rocked through me—I clenched around his cock and Priest swore low and sexy in my ear. Then, he slowly pulled out nearly all the way before slamming his cock back in, hard enough to rock me up the bed. Hard enough that I felt it in my throat.

Priest didn't hold back after that. He fucked me hard and fast, dragging his cock almost all the way out and then slamming back in, each time driving it against that spot inside me that sent pleasure racing up my spine. I cried out with each thrust, rocking my hips back to meet him and then forward into the grip of his fist. Fuck, it was so good—and the heat of his breath against my skin, and his sporadic sloppy kisses, made it even better.

"Fuck," Priest groaned as he pounded into me. "Fuck, Mal, I'm gonna come."

"Yeah," I said, and I was drooling onto the pillow, so overwhelmed and lost in the sensation. "Come on, want to feel it."

"Christ, the mouth on you," Priest said. He straightened up, gripped my hip hard in one hand and jerked my cock with the other as he buried his cock in me a half-dozen more times. Then, with a loud, shuddering moan, he came. His cock throbbed inside me, and his grip around my cock went loose and sloppy.

I didn't need much, though. The sensation of Priest coming inside me—knowing that I was the one to make him lose control like that—was so fucking good. I wrestled one hand beneath me, tangled my fingers with Priest's, and guided his grip. It took only a few more strokes before the intense pleasure that had raced through me was building, and building, like a wave, or a storm.

"Fuck, *Priest,*" I cried out, drawing out the syllable of his name into a moan as I spilled all over his hand and onto my sheets.

"Goddamn," Priest murmured as he pulled out. He disposed of the condom, and then flopped on the bed, uncaring of the wet spot there.

With some effort, I lowered myself to lie down on the bed as well. I felt loopy, a little spacy—he'd fucked me so hard I could barely make sentences.

Priest rolled onto his side next to me and grinned. He looked gorgeous—flushed with exertion, his blue eyes glimmering happily, his salt-and-pepper hair messy with sweat. "You all right?" he asked, half-teasing and half-concerned.

"Jeez," I said. "How the fuck am I going to ride my bike after that?"

Priest barked a surprised laugh. He maneuvered me onto my side, facing away from him, and then slotted up against me so his chest was pressed to my back again. He wrapped his arms snugly around me and then dropped a kiss to my shoulder. It was so sweet and cozy—a delicious counterpoint to the rough, passionate way he'd fucked me just moments before.

"I'll give you a massage," he said. "I think you'll survive."

"We can't sleep," I muttered. "It's the middle of the afternoon."

"We can sleep for a little while," Priest protests. "Not like there's anything on the schedule."

"Hm," I said. "Maybe just for a little while."

"Then we'll shower," Priest said, "and then go downstairs and let the enforcers tease us."

I laughed, then folded my hands around Priest's forearm where he was holding me close. That did sound good. A nap, a shower, then hanging with the club—enduring their good-natured teasing.

It sounded almost too good.

Because despite how intense and passionate the sex had been, it hadn't felt like just sex. It'd felt... it'd felt like more than that. Like making love.

I knew it was just because we had such a strong friendship—the foundation of trust and mutual respect was there. It wasn't *love*, not in a romantic way. It was just an extension of our history together. And even though I *knew* that, I couldn't shake the feeling that it'd *felt* different. Like more, and in a way that *didn't* make me want to run.

Priest's breathing evened out behind me, and I tried to do the same. But despite how exhausted my body was, my mind started running in circles. No matter what happened, I couldn't fall for my best friend. Not when we'd so carefully established the boundaries around this—whatever *this* was.

I wasn't going to risk our friendship. And I wasn't going to ask Priest to give me something he wasn't ready to give. He might not *ever* be ready, and I didn't want to put that kind of pressure on this. Because where there was pressure, there was potential for breaking. Our friendship was the most important thing. I'd prioritize that over my confused feelings any day.

And yet, as his arm tightened around me in sleep, something inside me ached.

Chapter 19 - Priest

"Ugh." Mal grimaced at his phone, squinting in the dim morning light.

It'd been a few days since we'd finally had sex, and since then, I couldn't keep my hands off him. It hadn't lessened my desire at all—if anything, the sex had only made my desire stronger. I wanted to spend every moment I could with him. We didn't spend every night together—our schedules were too busy for that—but I savored the nights we did. Like last night. Waking up with Mal in *my* bed, in *my* cabin, felt almost too good to be true.

"What is it?" I asked. I rolled over onto my belly and swung my arm over Mal's middle, then pressed my nose into his shoulder. He was flat on his back, holding his phone above his face as he scrolled through it. "Bad news?"

"No, just the usual," he grumbled. "An update on who my enforcement detail is tomorrow." He sighed and tossed his phone carelessly aside onto the mattress. "Getting pretty sick of being followed around like this, I gotta say."

I blew a raspberry onto his shoulder. "Sucks being president, doesn't it?"

"Feel like I'm being babysat," Mal grumbled.

I laughed. He wasn't used to the enforcement detail the way I was—the Elkin Lake chapter had dealt with a lot more violence, both historically and recently, and I was pretty used to being followed around by enforcers. Even though Mal lived in the motel, he was used to being able to get a few hours alone by taking his bike somewhere. And that simply hadn't been safe over the past few weeks. He was starting to feel a little antsy—and trapped.

"You're cute when you're whiny," I said, circling my hand on his ribs.

"What?" Mal squawked. "You can't call a fifty-four-year-old man *cute.*"

"Sure, I can," I teased. "When it's *true*. Look at you pouting about being babysat."

"I'll show you cute," Mal grumbled, and before I could react, he wrestled out from under my arm and bodily shoved me off the bed.

Now it was my turn to squawk, flailing as I slid off the mattress, taking half the comforter with me. "Hey!" I said through my laughter, flat on my ass between the mattress and the wall. "Surprise attack! Not fair!"

"Well-deserved," Mal said as he climbed out of bed himself. Of course, he didn't come over to check and help me up, he just cackled and descended the stairs—for coffee, I assumed, as that was always his top priority in the morning. I should've known better than to tease a pre-coffee Mal.

I climbed to my feet, still shaking my head and chuckling to myself, even as my butt ached where I'd landed on it. Things were *so* good with Mal. Moments like this were especially good. The simple domesticity of it, and the playfulness, were quickly becoming the parts of my day I looked forward to most.

Of course, part of me still itched a little about the boundaries we'd set. We claimed to just be friends with benefits, but in moments like this, when I woke up with Mal in my arms, it didn't *feel* like friendship. It felt like so much more. I wasn't ready to delve into that too deeply, though. And I didn't want to scare Mal away by asking what exactly *he* thought was going on.

He'd made it clear he wasn't keen on commitment, and I'd agreed—I wasn't ready. Just because moments like this felt intimate in a way that I was beginning to crave didn't mean either of us wanted to define this as something *more*. This was simply what happened when you added sex to thirty years of friendship.

Sometimes it felt like I was waiting for the other shoe to drop. But I chalked that up to my own fears, and my own grief—it wasn't rooted in reality. If Mal was happy taking things one day at a time, I was too. That was better for us both, and it was *working*. No use trying to fix what wasn't broken.

I tugged on my boxers, discarded carelessly last night, and then descended the stairs to the intoxicating smell of fresh-brewed coffee—and the more intoxicating sight of Mal standing at the coffeemaker, naked, with a mug in his hand and a blissed-out expression on his face.

I wolf-whistled, low, and Mal didn't open his eyes. "Don't say a word," he said.

"But you look so—"

"Don't," Mal interrupted warningly, but he couldn't stop the smile from spreading across his face.

"Don't what?" I teased. I stepped close and slid my hand across his lower back, barely brushing my fingers over the swell of his ass. "Talk about how cute your ass is?"

"That's exactly what," Mal said. "You better watch it before I don't let you touch this ass ever again."

"Hm, don't think you'd be able to resist me," I said, then dropped a kiss on his neck. I reached overhead and pulled a mug from the cabinet then poured myself a cup of coffee, too.

Mal took a sip and peered at me over the top of his mug. "Yeah? Want to test that theory?"

"You should be nice to me," I teased. "I'm starting to feel like I shouldn't give you your surprise at all."

Mal raised his eyebrows. He leaned his hip against the counter, mug still in hand, eyes tracking me as I fixed my coffee the way I liked it (no sugar, hint of cream). He looked so good like this, naked in my kitchen, all that gorgeous dark skin on display, from the curve of his biceps to his muscular thighs to his ankles crossed casually as he leaned.

Desire swirled low in my gut—but it wasn't just his naked body that did it. It was the sight of him like this in *my* kitchen, comfortable and teasing, like he belonged. Like we did this all the time.

"Surprise?" Mal asked. "What's the occasion?"

"Does there have to be an occasion just for me to do something nice?" I teased.

Something in Mal's expression softened. "Well, when you put it like that. It's just been a while since someone's gotten me a surprise." He grimaced. "Other than bad, stalker-related surprises."

"Yeah, the whole stalker deal is part of the reason I wanted to do this. I know you've been stressed about it—and feeling a little irritated by the constant enforcement tail."

"Is it that obvious?" Mal asked, rubbing his face.

"Uh, yes?" I said with a laugh. "It's literally the first thing you said this morning."

Mal cringed. "Well, in my defense—"

"—it was before you had your coffee," I finished for him. "I know. It's fun to tease you when you're all grumpy."

"That's why you got shoved off the bed," Mal said matter-of-factly.

"So," I continued, as if he hasn't spoken, "I cut a deal with Blade."

Mal looked interested now. "What kind of deal?"

"We're ditching the babysitters and going for a ride," I said.

He brightened. "Ditching the sitters? No way. How'd you swing that?"

"Raven put some fancy tracking thing on our phones, and we have to have it activated the whole time, and we have to stick together," I said, parroting off the rules that Blade had given me. It hadn't been too hard to convince him to agree to it, though—he knew how irritated Mal was getting, and this was a good compromise to give us both a breath of privacy. "So no running off on your own, agreed?"

"I don't think there's any risk of that," Mal said.

He beamed, then set his mug down. I did the same, just in time for him to fling his arms around my neck. I wrapped my arms around his waist, tugging him close as he kissed me.

"Thanks," he murmured into my mouth. "I really, really need this."

I savored the feeling of his bare chest pressed to mine, his soft cock against my hip, his lips parting sweetly against my mouth. Seeing him so happy made my heart pound, like fireworks were exploding in my chest. It was an addictive feeling. I wanted to make him this happy, over and over. Wanted to keep giving him gifts like this. He deserved to have someone who took care of him—and I wanted that someone to be me.

I pushed that thought away. One day at a time. And today was supposed to be a day for Mal to relax. The fact that I got to go with him only made it better.

*

MAL

We got dressed in a hurry, exchanging heated kisses between pulling on our clothes. Part of me wanted to chuck Priest onto the bed and show him how grateful I was with a knockout blowjob, but the draw of the open road—sans enforcers—was too powerful. And that was saying a lot, because my recent desire for Priest was a force to be reckoned with.

Outside the cabin, I glanced around, shocked that there weren't any enforcers waiting to follow us. "Wow. We're really allowed to be alone, huh?"

"Just for a few hours, yep," Priest said, and grinned. He looked so fucking sexy in his riding gear: fitted jeans, well-worn boots, and his leather jacket zipped up over his broad chest. "Let's not waste it."

First, we stopped by Pepper's Pizza and picked up sandwiches for lunch later, then made our way outside of Junee and onto the winding two-lane highways. The further we got away from Junee, the more the roads widened and the traffic dissipated, until it was just the roar of our bikes, the road, the clear blue skies, and the brisk air. It felt incredible to just get out and ride with no real destination, to have nothing to worry about other than the engine beneath me and the asphalt ahead.

Sometimes I pulled ahead, taking us onto familiar winding roads I loved to ride, and other times Priest led, guiding us to his favorite back roads. But the best moments were when the highway widened and we could ride side by side.

It felt different, riding with Priest. Felt even better than riding alone—and that surprised me. I savored my alone time, craved it even. But having Priest at my side didn't feel like an invasion of my private time at all. We just… fit.

I shook away that thought. We fit because we'd been friends for such a long time, and the sex had made our friendship even closer. *Of course*, I enjoyed his company. These feelings weren't anything more than that—just gratitude for his friendship and thoughtfulness. I didn't need to get greedy and start wanting more than Priest was able to give me—and I didn't need to risk ruining this friendship, either.

And it wouldn't just potentially ruin our friendship, either. Was I ready to want more, only to have it taken away later? Was I ready to risk that kind of pain again?

Ahead, Priest whistled and nodded toward an exit. I followed him as he led us back toward Elkin lake, to the familiar highways that led to the lake itself. But instead of taking me to the lake, we went up. And up. And up. We pushed our bikes up the narrow, switchbacking highway, with Priest in the lead. It'd been a long time since I'd gone this high up in the mountains, despite having lived near Elkin Lake for so many years. Priest led us onto a narrow gravel road with no signage. The road ended abruptly, and the tree line opened up, and we were at…

An overlook. One I'd never been to before. We were so high in the mountain, the air felt a little thin. The overlook was a small, grassy area, with a view of the dark blue, still lake and the open sky dotted with clouds. It was gorgeous. I thought I'd seen all that Elkin Lake had to offer, and yet this view took my breath away with its beauty.

Just when I thought I had everything understood and sorted out—something new to surprise me. The same lake, from a different vantage point, looked completely different. Inspired new feeling in me. And when I looked at Priest, I felt something similar.

"Come on," Priest said, pulling out the sandwiches and chilled beers from Pepper's. "Let's enjoy the privacy while we've got it."

I spread out a blanket on the grass and we sat together on the overlook. Before eating, I sighed heavily and leaned back onto my elbows, tilting my head back to enjoy the crisp air and the sunshine. God, it was nice to sit here and not feel the eyes of the enforcers on my back the entire time.

Priest's phone dinged in his pocket. He fished it out and then grinned at the screen.

"Who is it?" I asked, opening my eyes just enough to see him.

"Raven," he said. "He's probably on tracker duty. He's just checking in to make sure we're okay." Priest tapped out a quick response, then set his phone on the blanket beside him. "Sometimes that boy makes me wonder who the parent is in the relationship, with how overprotective he gets."

"Dante's the same way," I said with a chuckle. "You'd think I wasn't the one to change his diapers all those years. Gotta admit, though, he's grown up pretty smart."

"Course he did. He's like his dad."

I scoffed and knocked my foot against Priest's. "Watch out, you're gonna inflate my ego even more." Then my phone dinged with a notification, startling me.

Priest laughed. "Who's on your back, now?"

"Probably Dante," I said as I unlocked my phone. "Oh," I said with some surprise when I looked at the screen, "not Dante, my other child."

"Tru?"

"The one and only." I shook my head fondly. "He's being nosy but trying to play it off like professional sergeant-in-arms interest."

"Funny how that's happened," Priest said. "It's like I woke up one day and had twenty children."

"I know," I said with a shake of my head. "Glad I didn't have to change all those diapers."

Priest barked a laugh. "Good point." He smiled and scooted a little closer. "The older I get, the more protective I feel of all of them, though. And proud. Even though Blade's the president, I can't help but see him as my son. I just try not to come off as condescending when I offer advice."

"You don't, don't worry," I said. And it was true—Priest had the most experience out of anyone in the Elkin Lake chapter, but when he offered advice, it never came off as patronizing. It was a balance I tried to mimic as president myself, but I didn't quite have the warmth that Priest did.

"I'm just glad I'm not president," he admitted with a smirk. "No offense."

"None taken," I said. "You're not wrong, it's a lot of work. Not that vice isn't, I mean—"

"I know," Priest said. "It's just different. I just don't have the energy to direct the club anymore, you know? Better to let the next generation take the reins, at least in our chapter."

"I have a feeling it'll be something similar for the Junee chapter pretty soon," I admitted. "I think Dante wants my job."

"He'd be a hell of a good president," Priest agreed. "Maybe Tru as vice?"

"Oh, God," I groaned at the thought. "They'd burn the place to the ground. We need someone with sense in the inner circle."

"Okay, Nix, then," Priest said through his laughter. "He'd keep the insanity contained."

I paused and nodded thoughtfully. "Honestly, you might be onto something with that."

"What can I say?" Priest said. "I'm a man of ideas." Then he leaned over, wrapped his hand around my nape, and tugged me in for a kiss. "I think you should stick around as president for a while, though. I'm getting kind of used to it."

I smiled into the kiss. "Don't worry, you're stuck with me for at least a few more years."

"Good," Priest said. We traded lazy kisses for a long few minutes. It was so good—a reprieve from the stress of the past few weeks. All I had to worry about was the chilly breeze rustling through the trees, and the warmth of Priest's mouth on mine.

Sometimes I was overwhelmed by how lucky I was to live a life like this—with a supportive club, children, and a plan for the future. Having Priest here, being not just a friend but a source of comfort and stability and companionship, felt like it was almost too much. Like I didn't deserve it— like I couldn't be the kind of man that Priest needed, especially after losing Ankh.

But there was no point in worrying about that now. Not when the day was so beautiful, and Priest was smiling into the kiss, and we hadn't even broken into our sandwiches.

Chapter 20 - Priest

It was a clear Saturday afternoon, a few days after my outing to the overlook, and I, for once, had nothing on my schedule. Jonah and Maverick were both working at Ankhor Works, so I was on duty babysitting Grace; Gunnar, Blade, Logan, Raven, and a handful of other members were working together preparing for a cookout tomorrow.

I bounced Grace on my lap, where I was lounging on the couch. She laughed at the motion, alternating reaching for me, and getting distracted by Gretel's yipping in the kitchen.

"Come on, Gretel, chill out," Logan said with a laugh as he nearly tripped over the dog. "No snacks for you in here."

The dog whined indignantly in response.

From the open back door, Coop's whistle filtered through. "Gretel! Quit causing problems!"

Gretel bounded outside, careened off the porch steps, and started rocketing around the backyard, which led to some aggrieved shouting from Rebel, who was currently manning the grill.

"So." Blade wiped his hands on a kitchen towel, leaving Logan to tend to the chili they were preparing in the crockpot. "How was your date earlier this week?"

My face flushed. "It wasn't a date."

"That sounds like something someone who went on a date would say," Logan said with a smirk.

"He's got you there," Gunnar said, though he kept his attention on the celery he was chopping.

"It was fine," I said.

"Ooh," all the guys said in unison.

I rolled my eyes. "Mal really needed a day off from the constant enforcement tail, he's not used to that," I said. Grace fidgeted, looking a little bored and irritated. I stood up and walked over to the kitchen, bouncing her in my arms. "It was good for him—for us—to get a little privacy amidst all this craziness."

"So it *was* a date," Raven said.

"You're missing the point," I said with a shake of my head.

"Not sure he is," Blade said, suddenly serious. "You know it's okay if it was a date, right?"

"Yeah," Gunnar said. "You two are being cagey for no reason."

"I'm not being cagey," I said, even though Gunnar was right. I peered at Grace. "Am I being cagey, Gracie?"

She blew a raspberry.

"There's your answer," Logan said.

"Your business is your own," Blade said, "but you know, whatever direction your relationship with Mal takes... We all support you. Right, guys?"

"Of course," Gunnar said. "Still want to know the details, though."

"That's because you're nosy," Raven said demurely without looking up from his laptop.

Blade looked meaningfully at me but didn't ask outright.

I sighed. "Well," I said, keeping my gaze focused on Grace, because that was easier than meeting the eyes of the curious club members in the kitchen. "I mean, we've been friends for a long time."

"Right," Raven said.

"So it's different," I said, even as my face flushed. "It's easy to—to get close, because there's years of history between us. So being friend with benefits has helped us get closer, too, in a way."

"Closer?" Blade prompted.

"It's…" I sighed. "It's complicated. We're taking it one day at a time."

I wasn't ready to talk to the guys about my feelings for Mal, because I didn't fully understand them myself. How much of this was friendship? How much was just having sex after a long time without it? And—how much of it was *real*? It was too much to think about. It still made my gut swoop with anxiety, and guilt.

Grace made a pinched face and started squirming in my arms. Well, I was saved, because that was a familiar smell, and one that I wasn't too keen on dealing with myself. I'd changed more than enough diapers in my time, thank you very much. "Gunnar, this girl needs a change, you want to handle that?"

"Sure," Gunnar said. He set the knife down, abandoning his chopping task to scoop Grace out of my arms and take her upstairs to one of the available guest rooms that doubled as a nursery when she was here. And, well, that wasn't the reaction I was expecting. Not from Gunnar, who had been openly terrified of Grace when she'd first come into our lives.

I blinked at Raven as Gunnar disappeared up the stairs. "What just happened?"

"Oh, now it's Priest's turn to pry," Blade said with a grin. "Let's go check on how this meat for the chili's coming along." He hooked a finger in Logan's belt loop and guided him outside to bother Rebel and Coop.

"So?" I asked, sliding into the seat next to Raven. "What's that about? Gunnar's suddenly not afraid of toddlers?"

"Maybe Grace is just especially non-threatening," he said primly as he closed his laptop.

"Oh, is that it?" I asked.

Raven smiled, small, and a little nervous. "We've been talking about it."

My heart somersaulted. "About what?"

"Having a baby," Raven admitted. "Either using a surrogate or adopting—we're not sure yet. We're still just talking about it. And—" he sighed and squared his shoulders a little bit. "I know it's fast, but I've known Gunnar my whole life, he's my best friend, the love of my life—it just feels like the right time."

"I don't think it's too soon at all," I said. I was still reeling—*my son*, considering a *child*. I could hardly believe it.

Raven slumped a little in relief. "Really?"

"Really," I said. I took his hand in mine. "I'm so proud of you. And Gunnar, too. I can't believe he's changed his tune."

"It was Grace that did it," Raven admitted. "She really showed him that there wasn't anything to be intimidated by. He's great with her."

"He really is," I said with a shake of my head. "Never thought I'd see the day."

"He's it for me," Raven said a little dreamily. "He's everything. And I want to start a family with him. The way you did with Dad."

"You deserve that," I said, and I meant it. Raven finding love like I'd found with Ankh was one of the greatest joys of my life.

"And," Raven said tentatively, "maybe you could have that again, with Mal."

I started, pushing back in my seat a little. This was not where I was expecting this conversation to go. "Now, you know I wouldn't be doing anything at all with Mal if you didn't support us, but I'm not intending to get that serious with him."

"Good luck with that," Gunnar said as he descended the stairs with a freshly changed and happily chattering Grace in his arms. "I didn't intend to get serious with Raven, either. And here we are now."

"Where's here?" Raven teased.

"Planning a kid," Gunnar admitted. "If you told my twenty-year-old self this was where I'd end up, I'd've laughed in your face."

"Well, fatherhood looks good on you," I said with a smile. "And I can't deny that I've always wanted to be a grandfather."

"This kid's gonna be so spoiled," Raven said.

"Damn right," I said.

Gunnar dropped a kiss on top of Raven's head, then stepped into the kitchen with Grace chattering on his hip to stir the chili while Blade and Logan were outside. Raven flushed and smiled before he returned to his laptop. My heart clenched with love watching them interact—there was so much casual intimacy and love and trust there, and I knew they were ready to be parents.

Raven's comment lingered in my mind, though. Did he really expect that Mal and I would end up in a relationship comparable to the one I'd had with Ankh? He didn't think it was wrong for me to have a relationship like that again? He *wanted* that for me?

I could see his point, though. If I was ever going to have the kind of connection I had with Ankh, it'd have to be with someone who knew me—who had been through the trials of the last few decades, too. And Mal had. So it made sense that Raven would assume we'd connect in that way.

Even if it made sense, though, I didn't know if I was ready. To be with Mal in that way would be to open myself up to loss again—and I didn't know if I'd survive another. It felt safer to keep a little distance between us, to keep myself from getting too attached.

My phone dinged with a new notification, surprising me out of my reverie.

"Who could that be?" Raven teased.

"It's not Mal," I said with laugh. It wasn't a number I recognized, actually. I figured it was one of the prospects getting in touch, or a client from Ankhor Works, so I swiped open the message.

It wasn't either of those things, though. It was a video message. It looked like it'd been recorded in secret—from a high angle, in the unmistakable green tinge of night vision. In the video, Mal was sprawled out on the mattress, flat on his back with his head tipped back in pleasure. Xavier was riding him, his pale, narrow body writhing as he fucked himself onto Mal's cock. He glanced up at the hidden camera and smirked—and then the footage ended.

My stomach turned.

The flood of emotion was sudden and overwhelming. First, disgust—disgust that this awful man had gotten to know Mal in such an intimate way, without Mal even realizing who he was being so intimate with. And then anger that Xavier had used that intimacy to violate Mal. Recording him without his knowledge. It sickened me, and made me want to burn something to the ground in retribution.

How long had he been holding on to this footage? Who else might he have sent it to? Mal would be fucking crushed if this got out—he was already struggling with so much anger and embarrassment around this situation, and this level of violation and exposure would only make it worse.

And then, to my shame, I also felt *jealous*.

That certainly wasn't right. This wasn't about me—I had no right to feel jealous that Mal had slept with other guys. We weren't together in that way, and he didn't owe me monogamy, not to mention that this was before we'd ever even considered anything together. But I hated seeing him with another guy. Hated it all the way down to my core. Hated it in a way that made it suddenly very obvious how I felt about Mal.

I didn't want him to sleep with other guys. I wanted him to be *mine*.

But I couldn't worry about that now. That knowledge was overwhelmed by my anger and desire for justice—I wanted to kill this little fucker. How *dare* Xavier record this? And how dare he hang on to it until he found a way to get it to me?

Then, I realized, with a chill—he'd sent it *especially to me*. Targeted. He wanted me to see it, specifically. He obviously had suspicions, somehow, that Mal and I were together, and he was trying to get under my skin. Or trying to prove his deluded idea that he and Mal had 'something special.' When really it was one casual, meaningless fuck. Not like what Mal and I had.

Which was… what? Did it *have* meaning?

I shook off that feeling. Clearly, Xavier was still fucking with us. The DNA results hadn't come through conclusively yet, and since they hadn't, the cops hadn't been able to arrest him for breaking the restraining order. We hadn't seen him around Junee or Elkin Lake at all, but he was obviously still out there. The enforcers seemed to be cooling off a little—not shirking their duties, but relaxing, thinking that Xavier wouldn't chance coming for Mal again with the police closing in on proof.

"Pops?" Raven asked. "Everything okay?"

"Where's Blade?" I stood up. "Blade! Get in here!"

Gunnar's eyes narrowed. "What happened?"

"It's Xavier," I said, low. "I've about had enough of this shit."

Blade, Logan, Rebel, and Coop stepped inside from the backyard. As soon as Blade saw my expression, the smile fell off his face. "Priest? What's going on?"

"Xavier's sending *me* messages now," I said. "He's fucking with us."

"What kind of messages?" Blade asked sharply.

"Videos," I said, angrily. "Of him and Mal."

"He recorded *videos*?" Raven asked. "Secretly?"

"Yeah," I said, grimacing. The anger was building, growing like a flame inside me. "Fucking *violating*. And then sending it to me to get under my skin? He's escalating even when we've got our shit on lockdown."

"That's fucking disgusting," Coop said. "What an asshole."

"More than an asshole," I said. "This is unconscionable. I'm not going to fucking wait around anymore while he toys with us. He's winding up to something, and I'm not about to let Mal get caught in the crossfire of it. What the *fuck* are the cops doing?"

"These things take time," Rebel said apologetically. "But doing things the right way is the only way to ensure he's put away for good. The worst outcome would be not having enough evidence, and he walks."

"I'm sick of waiting!" I barked. We'd done everything the right way: gotten the restraining order, let the cops into the motel, established our enforcement tails, sat on our hands while the cops took their sweet time testing the evidence. And the whole time Xavier was just out there, biding his time. Walking free. "He's not just sending texts anymore, he's got *video*. Who knows what else he has? Who he might send shit to? He's got to be planning something, and I'm not going to wait to find out what it is. I think we're overdue for some club justice."

"Priest," Blade said. "We agreed that wasn't the route we were taking here. *Mal* agreed."

"I don't need him to know," I said. I was impulsive, dizzy with rage. I just wanted to get my hands on this fucker—

this asshole who was making Mal's life hell. He deserved better than that. And I was going to make it happen. "This is personal now."

"Don't be crazy," Gunnar said. "Even if it's personal, it's still club business."

"Pops, you don't even know where he is," Raven said.

"Come on," Rebel pleaded. "The cops are close."

"I'll find him," I said, then turned on my heel and headed toward the door. I didn't need the guys' approval, not right now, not when I was being driven ahead purely by anger and disgust and not a small amount of possessiveness.

As I approached my bike, though, a familiar engine rumble cut through the silence. Mal pulled up next to me, cut off the engine, then pulled off his helmet to reveal his easy smile.

"Hoped I'd catch you here," he said. But then his brow furrowed. "What's wrong?"

Some of my anger dissipated in the face of his concern. With a sigh, I pulled out my phone and showed him the video message.

"Shit," he said. His voice was quiet, and his face went slightly pallid as he watched, eyes wide. "This just showed up on your phone?"

"Yeah," I said. "Unknown number."

"That *fucker*," Mal growled. "I should've known he'd have something like this."

"You didn't know he was recording?" I asked. I didn't think so—but I needed to be sure.

"Of course not!" Mal said. "It was a random fling. I don't need a recording of that. But it makes sense now that he'd do that. And keep it in his back pocket like this. Jesus." He rubbed his forehead. "This just keeps getting worse and worse."

My blazing anger faded again, settling into a low burn, like coals. Not so urgent anymore. Seeing Mal's face fall made it suddenly obvious what was more important right now— *supporting* him. He didn't need me to go out and throttle Xavier, no matter how much I wanted to. That was what *I* wanted to do. But that wasn't what he *needed*.

What he needed was a friend.

"Come on," I said. "Let's go to my place. Have a beer. Talk about what to do."

Blade stepped out onto the porch, looking like he was about to yell after me, but when he saw Mal and me together, he snapped his jaw closed. "Hey, Mal."

"Blade," Mal said with a nod.

"So, Priest, change of plans?"

I cringed. "Yeah, uh. We're going to go to my place."

"What were the plans originally?" Mal asked.

"Priest was on his way to find Xavier and beat his ass," Gunnar said, appearing behind Blade with a smirk on his face. "Regardless of the club's opinion on that."

"I still want to," I admitted.

Mal patted my shoulder. "Glad I caught you, then. That'd only make things worse." His expression darkened. "Who knows what he's capable of?"

"You don't think I could take him?" I asked, half-teasing, half-serious.

"I don't think he'd fight fair," Mal said gruffly. "After all this shit he's pulled, I don't know what to expect."

"All right," Blade said. "As long as you're not going to run off and chase him down."

"Not right now, at least," I said.

"I'll take that," Gunnar said.

I knew I'd be talking to the sergeants-in-arms about my almost-defection a little later, but for now, I'd take their grace—we all knew that Mal's safety was the most important thing. I wrapped my arm around his shoulder, tugging him close as I led him down the path toward my cabin. Because that's what I wanted, even more than I wanted to see Xavier brought to justice.

I wanted Mal close.

Chapter 21 - Mal

The grainy, green-tinted video stopped playing, ending on a frame of Xavier smirking up at the hidden camera. Before I could stop myself, I wound it back and played it again. Regardless of how many times I watched it, it never changed: same footage of me on my back, unaware I was being recorded, caught up in the sensation of fucking Xavier. Or *Stefan*, as I'd thought at the time. It just seemed so fucking ridiculous. What did he intend to do with this footage? Was it just to get under Priest's skin? Not like he could blackmail me with it—this wasn't something I *needed* to hide from the club, even if I hated for them to see it.

"God," I said. "I can't believe all this shit. Just from a single hookup at a club."

"Kind of an argument for monogamy, huh?" Priest said from the kitchen as he fished out two beers from the fridge. Then he paused. "Not that—"

"Nah, I know what you mean," I said, waving my hand dismissively. I knew Priest wasn't advocating for *us* to be monogamous—he'd made it clear he was happy with our friends-with-benefits relationship, and I was, too. It was definitely easier than hookups. "This drama has put me off Stallions, though. That much is for sure. I am way too old to be dealing with this."

"I'm sure they're mourning the loss down at Stallions," he teased. "First Jazz, now you? I bet they feel it in their finances."

He sat down on the couch next to me and offered me a beer. I took it gratefully.

I used to be all about monogamy, way back in the day. Melanie had been the center of my world. When she'd left me unexpectedly to be a single father, I'd decided that I wasn't going to put Dante's—and my own—stability at risk again by getting into another relationship. I didn't think I'd ever be able to trust again, not after Melanie had broken my trust so completely.

But that was thirty years ago. Dante had his own stability now, and I did too, in the club. And Priest was a big part of that stability. My commitment *against* commitment was obviously coming back to bite me in the ass. What was the point of keeping myself so alone now? What was stopping me from turning to Priest, letting him know what I was thinking?

What was I so afraid of?

Still, something held me back. I grimaced at the video.

"We both know that's not why he's obsessed with me. He's just fucked up. And I'm humiliated." I shook my head. "I can't believe he sent that to you. I'm sorry—sorry you had to see that."

I couldn't imagine how Priest must've felt seeing it. I would've been disgusted. Watching it, I couldn't believe I'd ever enjoyed sex with Xavier—but I had. I'd wanted him, at least physically. And my expression in the video was proof of that.

"Hey," Priest said gently. He took the phone out of my hand and put it aside, forcing me to stop watching the video. "You don't have anything to be sorry for."

"I'm the reason all this is happening," I said. "I never should've fucked around at Stallions."

"*You're* not the reason," Priest said seriously. "*He* is. *None* of this is your fault."

Then he closed the distance between us and kissed me. It was a slow, sweet kiss, with his hands folded over mine. My heart flipped somersaults in my chest. I was stunned he wanted to touch me, after seeing me with Xavier like that. But maybe—maybe he meant it. Maybe he really did believe it wasn't my fault.

Priest pulled away and tipped his forehead against mine.

"It made me so fucking mad seeing that footage," he admitted in a whisper. My heart sank, but before I could say anything, he pressed his lips together then said, "I was furious that he'd violate you like that. Recording without your knowledge. And I felt really—possessive. Like he didn't *deserve* to have footage of you. I just went into a rage."

"That's what made you want to go kick his ass?" I asked. "This footage?"

"Yeah," Priest said. "And I still do. I've postponed it, but I still want to kick his ass."

I smiled and huffed a laugh. I'd agreed to do this the legal way, following Rebel's instruction, but honestly...

something about having Priest all fired up and wanting to fight for me turned me on. Made me feel cared for, that he wanted to defend my honor.

"I wouldn't be opposed to that," I said. "And, you know, I'm still president. So I get a say."

"Good," Priest said. "You'll have to help me plead my case to Gunnar. Later, though."

"Later?" I asked.

"Right now, I want to take care of you," Priest said. "Can I?"

My heart swooped in my chest. There was so much tenderness in his voice—it was different than the previous times we'd had sex. It didn't feel so playful. It felt like it meant something, and I wasn't sure what to do with that.

Before I could think about that too hard, he kissed me again, driving all the worries from my mind.

"Yeah," I murmured into the kiss. "Please."

This was exactly what I needed. Seeing the footage Xavier had secretly taken made me feel violated and used. Dirty. And Priest kissed me in a way that made it obvious he didn't think that was the case at all. He made me feel— *cherished*. Like what we had mattered. Like *I* mattered. He didn't want me for some deluded fantasy of what he thought I was, like Xavier did. He knew me—all of me. And still treated me with this much genuine sweetness and care.

Priest took my hand in his and guided me to my feet, and kept my hand wrapped in his as he led me up the stairs to his bedroom. There was no urgency in the motion, just promise. He was going to take care of me.

He tugged me across the threshold into the bedroom and closed the door behind us. I still partially expected him to kiss me like he usually did—with hunger and force and playfulness, starting a battle for dominance. But instead, he just set his hands at my hips and kissed me slowly and thoroughly. I sighed into the kiss, knees going a little weak and watery. Standing at the foot of the bed, Priest slowly pushed my jacket off my shoulders, then tugged my shirt overhead. He ran his hands over my chest attentively, adoringly, his touch light but intense as he traced the curve of my pecs, my waist, my abs.

"Get on the bed?" he asked. Then his fingers dipped into the waistband of my jeans. "And out of these?"

I nodded, breaking the kiss with some reluctance to shuck off my jeans and lie back into the bed. I folded my arms behind my head, comfortable in just my underwear as Priest stood at the foot of the bed, watching me. He ran his hand down my shin to my ankle, tracking the bone there, like he couldn't stand to have his hands off me for more than a few moments.

The affection of the gesture made desire roll through me, slow and heady. I'd never had a partner look at me this way: with so much intensity and desire and something deeper I wasn't sure how to name. His warm blue eyes traveled hungrily over my body. The way he looked at me made me feel sexy, desired, and I stretched a little on the bed, just to see the way his gaze followed the shifting of my abs.

Priest tugged off his own clothes quickly, tossing them carelessly aside until he was standing naked at the foot of the bed, with all that gorgeous muscle on display. He was so broad, barrel-chested, chest dusted with the same salt-and-pepper hair of his trimmed beard. I was already craving his touch again, the press of his chest to mine and the scratch of his beard on my skin.

My cock quickly got hard watching him strip so efficiently, and I palmed the shape of it idly through my underwear.

Priest's gaze darkened as he watched the motion. He said nothing, though, just stepped out of his own underwear, and I groaned at the sight of his cock already hard and hanging heavy between his legs. He grinned at the way it affected me and crawled onto the bed next to me. He rolled onto his side then ran his hand down my chest. With his palm flat, he touched me with delicious pressure, over my nipples and abs, making me hiss at the sensation.

God, my whole body sparked to life under his touch. It was overwhelming. The gentle but focused way he touched me reminded me of one of our first nights together, when he'd taken his time exploring my body from top to bottom, driving me crazy with every brush of his hands.

But this time there was more confidence in his touch. He knew how to drive me crazy now, knew the ways to touch me to make me fall apart under his hands.

He ran his palm over my cock, still trapped in my underwear. Even through the cotton, the sensation made me gasp—he pressed just hard enough and my cock throbbed in response, leaking enough precum to leave a dark stain at the front. Priest rubbed his thumb over the wet spot as he leaned over and kissed me again.

"Priest," I murmured, then shifted a little restlessly under his hands. "Please."

"What do you want?" Priest asked gently. He broke the kiss but only to drop feather-light kisses on my jawline, neck, collarbone, chest.

I sighed and tipped my head back in pleasure, then raked one hand through his thick hair. I wanted Priest to take control again, but in this new, gentle way. I wanted to lie back and let him have his way with me. Let him make me feel good.

"Want you inside me," I said.

"Yeah?" Priest asked. He kissed my chest again and then his lips curved into a smile against my skin. "I think that can be arranged."

He dragged his mouth a little lower, then dragged the flat of his tongue over my peaked nipple. I gasped at the sensation and tightened my grip in his hair. The pleasure jolted through me, and my hips bucked a little, like my body was already begging to get him inside me.

Priest pulled back, then slid my underwear over my hips, finally freeing my cock. He didn't touch it, though, not yet. Instead, he ran his hand over my shoulder, then down my side to my hip; he tugged, encouraging me to roll onto my side so we were facing each other.

"Like that," he murmured encouragingly. He rolled away just long enough to fish the lube out of his nightstand, and then he was close again, facing me on his side. It was such an intimate position, gazing at each other, and my heart pounded in my chest.

And not just with arousal.

Priest leaned forward and kissed me. Then he ran his hand down my thigh, kneading the muscle of my ass and my quad, before he hitched my leg up and over his hip. He kept kissing me. We were so close like this, so entangled, I felt lost in the sensation—safe, too, like I could let go of all my concerns and worries and just lean on Priest. It was so easy. He made everything so *easy*.

Then his touch disappeared and reappeared slick, sliding messily over my hip and then in between my ass cheeks to pet at my hole. With my leg hiked over his hip, I was open for his touch, exposed. The gentle way he maneuvered me and touched me made me feel drunk with slow, languid desire—I could stay like this for hours with him, trading wet, messy kisses as his slick fingers circled over my hole gently, promisingly. It wasn't enough to make me come, but it was relaxing in a way I wasn't used to sex being.

Just when I was about to beg for it, Priest finally pressed his finger slowly inside. I groaned into the kiss as he filled me—it was so slow, and so deliberate. The sensation was so heightened that I felt every slight movement all the way into my core. I groaned, shifting my hips back to meet his hand, and it wasn't long before Priest appeased me with a second finger, and then a third. He fucked his fingers into me deep and slow, taking his time stretching me out so there was no discomfort at all, just a rich, bone-deep sensation that had me sighing and moaning into the kiss.

I broke the kiss and tipped my head against his shoulder, gazing into the space between us. Priest's cock was huge and hard, lying against his thigh, and I wriggled my hand between us so I could wrap my hand around that enticing hot length. Priest exhaled at my touch, which turned into a moan as I began to stroke him slowly, twisting my wrist as best I could around the head to gather the slick precum in my palm.

"Fuck," Priest groaned, pushing his fingers somehow deeper inside me. "You want my cock?"

"Yeah," I murmured. "Need it."

Priest growled, then withdrew his fingers. He maneuvered me onto my back, and I spread my legs welcomingly, making space for him to settle between. He rolled a condom on quickly, and then settled between my legs. Despite how badly I wanted his cock, the need roaring through me, and the intensity of Priest's kiss, there was still no urgency. He was still taking his time. And that made it all the better.

He lowered down, resting his weight on one forearm beside my head, so he could keep kissing me, like he couldn't get enough. I tipped my hips up encouragingly. Desire ran molten through me, centered in the cradle of my hips; with his fingers gone, my body ached to be filled again. Priest gripped my thigh with his free hand, hiking it up and around his waist.

It was like our bodies just fit together. The head of his cock nudged against my hole, and then with hardly any resistance at all, he slid inside me.

"*Mal,*" Priest sighed, tipping his forehead against mine as he entered me. I wrapped my arms around his neck and pressed my fingers into the muscle of his lats. We panted into each other's mouths, in a facsimile of a kiss—his eyes were closed tightly, brow furrowed, sweat beading at his temple. Like the feeling of sliding into me was too good to stand.

And god, did it feel good for me, too. His cock was so hard, and so thick, and in this position it seemed to slide impossibly deep. I pulled him as close as I could, so we were chest to chest, and he buried his face in my neck, panting as he fucked into me.

He slid in slowly, inch by burning-hot inch, until he was sheathed fully inside me. I mouthed sloppy kisses at his temple as he panted against my skin, then skated my hands down the plane of his back to grip his ass hard. I squeezed the firm muscle there and Priest groaned—then I pressed forward, like I could push him even deeper inside me. God, it felt good, felt like his cock was made for me.

He got the hint, then lifted up just enough to capture my lips in another kiss as he began to move inside me.

He shifted his hips slowly, grinding into me more than thrusting, dragging his cock over my sweet spot with each movement. The pleasure burned low and intense inside me, slow-moving like honey, and I moaned into the kiss. As Priest began to thrust harder and deeper into me, the kiss devolved again, wet and sloppy as we gasped for breath together, tongues meeting.

"Priest," I moaned. "It's so good. So good."

"Yeah," Priest agreed breathlessly.

He released my thigh, but I kept my leg where it was, hitched around his waist. Priest worked a hand between us and wrapped it around my cock, and the sudden tight heat nearly sent me over the edge immediately. He began to fuck me a little faster, a little harder, and the pleasure intensified, rolling through me like waves from my core all the way to my toes curling in the sheets. I broke the kiss to toss my head back desperately, gasping his name.

My orgasm snuck up on me. It was like the heat rolling inside me suddenly flooded my body all at once, when Priest drove his cock into me just right as he simultaneously tightened his grip on the head of my cock. My core tightened, and I pulled Priest impossibly closer with my leg around his waist as my orgasm crashed through me. I came over Priest's hand, over my chest, and he jerked me through it until I was shivering with exquisite overstimulation.

"Fucking hell," Priest groaned. "You're so gorgeous when you come. And so fucking *tight*."

He mouthed a kiss at my neck as he grabbed my thigh again, tilting my hips up as he pounded into me faster, chasing his own release. It was right on the edge of too much, but it still felt good, intense and delicious as he fucked into me. I sank back into the mattress, pliant beneath him, and ran my hands up and down his back.

"Come on," I murmured into his ear. "Come inside me."

"Mal," Priest groaned, and pressed so deep inside me it made me gasp again, and then came. He shuddered through it, cock throbbing inside me.

Then with a heaving sigh, he collapsed onto me. The sudden weight made me exhale, surprised, and then I wrapped my arms around him. We stayed like that for a long few moments, wrapped up in each other, Priest still inside me. Finally, with a heaving groan, Priest lifted up and pulled out. I cringed a little at the sensation, and he kissed the expression off my face.

"Don't move," he said. "I'll clean us up."

He got to his feet and padded into the bathroom.

Then I was alone in the center of his big bed, still dizzy and flushed from the aftershocks of my orgasm.

It'd been *so* good. Impossibly good.

And we hadn't fucked like friends messing around. Face to face like that, wrapped around him… It was impossible to call it just sex this time. Just fucking. Just blowing off some steam. It was undeniably more than that.

Or at least it was for me.

Maybe it wasn't for Priest. There was no way to know. The way he treated me—it felt big. Important. Something that *could* be life-changing. But it *couldn't* be. We were taking care of each other, because we were friends. If Priest felt differently, he'd speak up about it, let me know, and it wasn't my business to push. The club relied on us too much to disrupt the status quo in such a huge way.

We'd decided to take things one day at a time, with no pressure, no expectations, and... I didn't know what this meant. But it felt scary. Like soon, it might hurt.

Priest emerged from the bathroom with a washcloth, clearly intending to clean me up again, but this time, I didn't think I could handle the tenderness. Not with this new, almost-painful knowledge twisting in my chest. Before he could climb onto the bed, I stood up and took the washcloth from his hand.

"Thanks," I said. "Just a sec."

"Sure," Priest said a little confusedly. He was just as surprised as I was that my legs worked.

I slipped into the bathroom and shut the door behind me. Then I braced both hands on the edge of the counter and took a deep breath, with my head bowed so I couldn't see my own kiss-swollen lips or the fresh hickeys on my neck and shoulder.

But I couldn't deny it. I couldn't play off this feeling like it was just the years of friendship between us.

I *loved* him.

And that thought terrified me. I could handle whatever Xavier had to throw at me, but this feeling... *this* I didn't know what to do with. All I knew was that I couldn't tell Priest. I'd promised I wouldn't ask him for anything serious—not when he was still grieving his husband. And I intended to keep that promise, no matter how much it hurt.

I cleaned up, rinsed my face, and then slid back into bed. Priest hummed happily and tugged me into his arms, slotting his chest against my back like it was the most natural thing in the world. "You okay?" he murmured into my nape.

"Yeah," I said. "Good night."

Priest inhaled and his grip tightened on me minutely, like he was about to say something. But he just sighed out the breath and murmured a goodnight as well.

Despite how exhausted I was, sleep wouldn't come. The realization was twisting me up in knots, and being in Priest's arms, knowing I shouldn't feel this way, knowing I couldn't have him the way I wanted, was too much to bear. I waited until his breaths evened out, and then slid out of his grasp. I dressed quickly and quietly. I just needed some fresh air. Needed some time alone to figure out what to do. And then I'd come back and sort this all out.

Chapter 22 - Priest

After what felt like just a few minutes of restless sleep, I woke up in an empty bed. "Mal?" I asked.

No response. The space beside me on the mattress was cold to the touch, and his clothes were gone. I sighed, rolled over and grabbed my phone. No messages from him either. It wasn't too late yet—just before eleven at night. I'd only slept an hour or so before realizing he wasn't here.

I wasn't surprised he was gone, though. Last night had been amazing—mind-blowing, even. Something had shifted between us, I'd felt it. It wasn't just sex anymore, even if that's all it had been up until that point. But it was more than that now. And I'd thought Mal felt it, too.

I knew him, though. I knew his moods, and the way he carried his anxiety in the tense line of his shoulders and the slight downturn of his full lips. And when I'd walked out of the bathroom, he'd had that anxious look on his face, and nearly fallen over in his hurry to stop me from cleaning him up. I'd almost asked what was up last night, with my arms around him, but I'd thought it'd be better to talk about it in the light of morning. When we both were a little more clearheaded, and not still reeling from the incredible sex we'd had.

Watching him fall apart beneath me last night, I'd known without a doubt that I was getting serious about him. That what I felt for him was beyond what I should feel in just a friends-with-benefits situation. All the qualities that had made me cherish him as a friend were still there: his warmth, his humor, his loyalty, and his kindness. But now, as our relationship deepened, I was discovering a new depth to *him* that I hadn't had the ability to delve into before. He was so sweet, and attentive, and thoughtful— and we had a shared connection to Ankh that made our friendship, and our relationship, even stronger.

Not to mention the sex was just getting better and better, the more we learned each other's bodies.

I sat up in bed. No way I was getting back to sleep—not now.

I'd never thought I'd feel this way for anyone again. I'd never thought there would be a man who would make me want to love again—I hadn't wanted to meet anyone. I'd thought Ankh was it for me. And yet here I was, longing for Mal. Wanting to be with him. Wanting to make this right, whatever it was. It wasn't the same love I'd felt for Ankh, but that didn't make it any less powerful, or any less meaningful.

Then I realized—*fuck*.

Mal was gone.

Alone. And we still didn't know where Xavier was. I trusted Mal to be able to defend himself, but my stomach turned at the thought of him alone at night.

I made a few quick calls. Mal wasn't at the clubhouse or the motel.

"Where would he have gone?" Gunnar asked tersely over the phone. "Raven's re-enabling the tracking, but it's going to take a little time. He didn't tell you where he was headed?"

"No," I said as I finished getting dressed and tugged my boots on. I opened the bottom drawer to my nightstand and peered thoughtfully at my handgun. Might as well. I tugged on the holster and set the gun at my hip. "But I think I have an idea."

Gunnar sent Coop and Siren to meet me outside my cabin. If Mal wasn't at either clubhouse, or any of the businesses, there was only one place he could be. I remembered the nights I'd caught him on the couch with a photo of Ankh in his hands. Both of us had leaned heavily on Ankh for advice, and sometimes, a photo wasn't enough. Sometimes I needed that sense of closeness. Needed to be somewhere private—somewhere I could talk to him.

Outside the cabin, I nodded gratefully at Coop and Siren. We hopped on our bikes and rode the short distance to the cemetery outside Elkin Lake. It was a chilly night, but the moon was bright and full in the sky, casting a gorgeous pale glow over the cemetery.

"You need us?" Siren asked as we parked.

"Hang back," I said with a nod. "If you don't mind."

They both nodded, lingering near the cemetery gates a respectful distance away as I followed the familiar path to Ankh's grave. Though the moonlight was bright enough to light the way, I hardly needed it. I'd walked this path so many times, I could do it with my eyes closed. Ankh was buried near the edge of the cemetery, close to tall old red river gum tree, so it felt private. He would've liked the view.

And there, leaning against his headstone just as I'd hoped, was Mal.

"Hey," I said.

Mal looked up, shocked. "Priest?"

"Thought I might find you here," I admitted. I half expected him to blow me off and say he needed some time alone, but he only sighed and rubbed his hand over his forehead.

"Needed some advice," Mal said.

"Yeah," I said. "I come here for that same reason."

He laughed a little and shook his head. "Am I that transparent?"

"I could tell something was wrong back at my place," I said. "I just wanted to make sure you were okay."

And I wanted to know what was going on—wanted to know how I could help him with this. I wanted him to know he didn't need to push me away.

Mal sighed and stood up. He looked exhausted. Even in the cool moonlight, I could see the slight bags under his eyes and the furrow in his brow—I wanted to kiss that expression of worry off his face.

"I'm sorry," he said.

"You don't have anything to apologize for," I said immediately. "I—I'm glad you came here. Glad I was right when I thought this might be where you were." I reached out and placed a hand gently on his shoulder. "What did you need advice on?"

Mal met my gaze. His dark eyes were warm, nervous but determined. "Us."

My heart leaped into my throat. "*Is* there an us?" I asked gently. "A real us? Because—"

A gunshot cracked through the still night air.

Before I could process what was happening, Mal gasped and collapsed forward into my arms. I staggered back, holding his weight up as ice-cold shock and terror ripped through me. Beneath my hand, pressed to Mal's back, sticky-wet warmth bloomed across his jacket.

Shouts behind me, steps as Siren and Coop ran toward me.

"He's mine!" Xavier shouted, wild-eyed, gun still drawn and shakily pointed at us. "We're supposed to be together! And he just threw me away? For some asshole like you? It's not fair! If I don't get to have him—"

He was still brandishing the gun, arm quivering, like he was preparing to take another shot. In my arms, Mal groaned as I pressed harder on the wound, trying to staunch the bleeding as best I could while still holding him up. Moving on autopilot, my other hand flew to my hip and grabbed my gun. Before Xavier could finish his sentence, I'd lifted my pistol, flipped the safety, and pulled the trigger.

And I had a lot of experience.

The shot hit Xavier in the center of the chest, and he staggered backward.

"Mal!" Coop shouted as he charged toward our side. Siren ran past us, gun drawn, toward Xavier's body crumpled in the grass.

"Oh my god," I whispered, as the reality of what had just happened began to hit. Mal shook in my arms as I slowly lowered us to the ground, so I was sitting up against Ankh's headstone with Mal cradled against my chest so I could keep applying pressure to the wound, even as my hand slipped on the wet leather. "It's not doing anything. Coop—"

"They're on the way," Coop said, already on the phone.

"Don't fucking die on me," I growled in Mal's ear. "You *can't*. You hear me? You hear what I'm saying?"

Mal exhaled hard. He was getting paler and paler, and his lashes fluttered against my neck as his breaths came hot, wet and labored. I could hardly breathe myself, could hardly see around the tears burning in my eyes. This couldn't be happening. I couldn't lose him. I wouldn't survive this kind of loss again.

Desperately, I tugged him closer. Coop pushed a balled-up piece of fabric into my hand—his shirt, I noted dully—and I pressed that against the wound with as much strength as I had. I knew it hurt, from the way Mal groaned, but that meant he was still alive. Still feeling it.

"Come on," I said. "Hang on. Stay with me."

After these painful years without Ankh, I'd finally opened my heart to someone else—I'd finally thought I could be happy again. And now the person I loved was going to be taken away from me again. Thoughtlessly. Meaninglessly. What was the point? I never should've brought Mal into my life like this. Never should've fallen for him at all.

If anything, this felt like a sign—a sign that getting involved with Mal this way had been a mistake. Everyone who I loved deeply, romantically with my whole heart, was taken from me. Violently and before their time. When—*if*—he survived this, I knew I couldn't keep going the way we had been. I couldn't risk getting closer to Mal. Couldn't risk suffering that pain again.

In the distance, sirens wailed.

In my arms, Mal went limp.

"No," I demanded brokenly, tugging him closer as my heart shattered. "Hang on, Mal. Just hang on."

Chapter 23 - Mal

Pain.

The pain dragged me out of unconsciousness first, throbbing, dull pain starting in my shoulder and radiating out to the rest of my body. I groaned, shifting restlessly on the mattress beneath me, unable to get comfortable.

Then I felt a hand on my ankle, encouraging me to stay still. Other sensations began to filter in, even though I kept my eyes closed: lights above me, low voices talking, the rhythmic *beep-beep-beep* of a monitor, the acrid smell of sterilizer.

"Hey, Dad," Dante said quietly.

With some effort, I opened my eyes. Dante was seated near the foot of the hospital bed with his hand resting gently on my ankle over the blanket. Heath stood behind him, concern on his face, his hand on Dante's shoulder. Blade was present, too, leaning against the wall with his arms crossed, and Priest sat in an armchair in the corner, his mouth set in a hard line, heavy bags under his eyes. He looked about as bad as I felt. And I felt really fucking bad.

I tried to meet his eyes, and Priest looked away.

What the fuck was going on? Anxiety rose in my chest, making my muscles tighten, which made the throbbing pain in my shoulder worsen. I winced again and tried to take a deep breath, but that hurt, too. I couldn't remember what had happened—why I was in the hospital—but Priest's reaction scared me even more. He never looked like this: closed off and distant.

My heart pounded in my chest.

Wasn't he worried? Didn't he care?

"What the fuck is going on?" I asked, turning my attention back to Dante. "What happened?"

"You were shot, Dad," Dante said. "You remember?"

It all came back in a rush. I remembered then, standing in the graveyard by Ankh's headstone. I'd gone there alone, to get some air and hopefully, with Ankh's help, figure out what I should do about my feelings for Priest. And then Priest had, to my shock, shown up. He'd known exactly where I'd run off to. Something about that had made it obvious to me that I needed to take the leap. To confess to him, damn the fear.

And then the white-hot pain had exploded across my back.

After that it was a blur—I remembered leaning heavily against Priest, trying to focus on the sound of his voice as I grew dizzier and dizzier, and dark spots danced in my vision. The last thing I remembered was Priest telling me to hang on—and then darkness.

"Yeah," I said shakily. "Yeah, I remember. It was Xavier, wasn't it?"

"It was," Dante said.

"Where is he?" I asked, anxiety ratcheting up again. "Is he still out there?"

"Calm down, Dad," Dante said, squeezing my ankle. "We got him."

"We?" I asked. So it was club justice?

"Priest did," Dante said. "He shot him."

"Died on-scene," Blade said. "It's over."

"Fuck," I said, relaxing a little into the mattress. "What about—"

"Self-defense," Dante said. "Multiple witnesses. Clear violation of the restraining order. It's fine."

I tried to meet Priest's eyes again, but he still wouldn't look at me. "*Fuck*," I said again. "So what the fuck happened to me?"

"The doctor said the bullet missed your heart by millimeters," Blade said. "You're lucky. Really fucking lucky."

"Took six hours of surgery," Heath said, looking pale.

"You lost a lot of blood," Dante added. "Recovery's not going to be easy."

"Shit," I said. No wonder I was so exhausted—six hours of surgery. I remembered, vaguely, the feeling of Priest's hand on my back. What if he hadn't been there to staunch the bleeding? What if Xavier had found me before Priest had?

Blade stepped a little closer.

"The cops were closing in on Xavier," he explained. "The DNA they'd managed to scrape up had finally come back a match, and there was a warrant out for his arrest for violation of the restraining order. Apparently that, combined with the knowledge that you and Priest were… spending time together, pushed him over the edge. From what we can piece together, he'd been following you last night."

"And I ran off alone," I said with a groan. "Giving him the perfect opportunity."

"That doesn't matter," Blade said. "What matters is that you're okay. And that Priest and the enforcers were there."

"The rest of the guys are texting a lot," Heath said, glancing down at his phone. "How are you feeling? Up for visitors?"

"Yeah," I said immediately. Even though I was exhausted, seeing the club members would reinvigorate me.

Priest stood up. "I'll go meet them in the lobby. Show them up to the room."

Before I could protest, he was gone. Heath and Blade both turned to their phones, giving Dante and me a moment of privacy. Dante scooted a little closer, then folded his hand over mine. He looked exhausted, his face pallid and eyes red-rimmed. He looked like he hadn't slept at all—he probably hadn't.

"You're really okay?" he asked.

"I am," I said. Even though I was exhausted, and hurting, and anxious about Priest's strange behavior—I was alive. Just a hair of difference in where the bullet had landed, and I wouldn't be here talking to my son at all.

It made me feel like someone was looking out for me. Like Ankh had known I still had more left to do—he'd protected me. The same way he'd always protected the club. Tears prickled behind my eyes, and I swallowed around the sudden knot in my throat. I squeezed Dante's hand.

"I'm sorry," I said. "I shouldn't have gone off on my own. Not after everything Xavier had done."

"It's all right," Dante said. "It was a mistake, but I think you've more than paid for it." He smiled weakly. "And you clearly needed... something."

"Yeah," I admitted. Priest stepped back into the room with a handful of anxious-looking members in tow. I met his eyes, and Priest offered me a small smile before he looked away again. "I think I still do."

Okay, well, it was more than a handful of members. Coop and Siren were there, of course, both looking as pallid as Dante did—clearly, they hadn't slept either. That made sense—they were the ones who'd been there when I'd been shot. They'd probably seen the whole thing.

"Mal," Siren said, hurrying to my side. "You're awake. How are you feeling?"

"Like shit," I said.

"Sounds about right," Coop said. He patted my leg, looking immensely relieved. "You scared us pretty bad there, Prez."

"Sorry, guys," I said. "I'm all right. Really."

After that, it was a rotating cast of members coming in with well wishes and, of course, food: Mav and Jonah with a card signed with a scribble by Grace, Tex and Jazz with takeout from Pepper's, Nix, Dawson, Brennan, Joker, Tru, Beau, Gunnar with relieved grins, and Raven with a tablet loaded with movies ready to watch—everyone. There were so many of us, no one could stay for long, because the nurse kept sticking her head in and telling us we were breaking the visitation rules.

"All right, all right," I said after the third time the nurse came in and gave me a stern look. "Y'all get going. I'll text if I need anything."

With a noisy chorus of well wishes, the members filed reluctantly out the door. Priest turned to leave, too. "Wait," I said.

He stopped.

"Priest, can I—can we talk?"

Dante glanced over his shoulder, the last one to leave. He nodded at me, eyes soft, and gently closed the door behind him.

Priest stiffened. For a moment I thought he might ignore me and walk out the door with the rest of the club, leaving me alone in the hospital room. But, to my relief, he sighed and turned around, then pulled a chair close to the side of my bed.

For the first time since I'd awoken in the hospital, I felt like I had his full attention.

"You know why I was at the cemetery in the first place?" I asked.

Priest sighed. I reached for his hand, and after a moment of hesitation, he took it and smoothed his thumb over my knuckles. The contact soothed some of my nerves. Maybe now that we were alone, we could—sort this out. Whatever it was.

"You said you needed some advice," Priest said. "That's where I go, too."

I swallowed. The prospect of talking to Priest about the way I felt—confessing to him—still filled me with anxiety, but after everything I'd been through, I was done beating around the bush.

"I was scared after we made love last night," I said.

Priest's expression softened, but then he pressed his lips into a hard line.

"I knew what I felt for you wasn't friendship anymore, or even anything appropriate for friends with benefits," I said. "I've been trying to pretend it is. For a while now. Trying to pretend like my feelings weren't changing. But they have been."

"Mal…"

"Then I thought I was dying," I said with a shake of my head. "And I realized in that moment, that all my hang-ups were so fucking… *trivial*. And I'd wasted so much time. I don't want to be friends with benefits with you, Priest."

Priest moved to pull his hand away, but I caught him and tightened my grip. Even that small motion made my wound twinge with a fresh burst of pain, and I grimaced.

"I love you, Priest," I said. "I'm *in* love with you."

For a brief moment, Priest's face opened into a soft expression I was more familiar with—kind, and caring, and warm. His lips parted, and he took a breath. "Mal," he said softly.

And I thought for a moment that maybe he would—

But then he tugged his hand out of mine. My heart skipped, and then sank.

Priest's face settled back into a stoic mask, his usually warm and attentive blue eyes unable to meet mine. His posture was stiff, and he had a deep furrow in his brow.

What had I expected?

I'd thought this experience would bring us together, in a terrible way. That Priest would have the same realization that I did—that we were wasting time dancing around each other, pretending not to want more, when we were so compatible. And when life was so short. But Priest didn't smile at me the way I was used to, nor did he lean closer, nor did he touch me at all.

"I'm so glad you're okay," Priest said. "I was really…" He sighed, sat back in his chair, and raked his hands through his hair. "I was really worried. I really thought we were going to lose you. And I'm so fucking glad we didn't."

There was a 'but' coming. My heart was in my stomach. This wasn't what was supposed to be happening. Not like this. "Priest, what—"

"It's not working," Priest said softly. "This arrangement. The friends-with-benefits thing. And I think we should go back to just being friends."

It was like I hadn't spoken at all.

"Just *friends*?" I asked incredulously.

"Yeah," Priest said. "I think that's best for us, and for the club."

He still wasn't meeting my eyes. I couldn't believe this. My chest was in knots, the pain worsened by the throbbing in my gunshot wound, and I felt like I'd had cold water dumped unceremoniously on me. Just friends? After all of this, I was supposed to back to pretending like nothing had changed between us?

This whole time, Priest hadn't felt anything for me? Nothing at all?

I was such a fucking idiot. I'd been right this entire time— there was no point in trying to commit again. Trying to find something real. Because right when I needed Priest most, he was leaving me behind. Just like Melanie had. Despite the club, I was truly on my own.

"Wow," I said, with a cold, shocked laugh. I turned my gaze to the ceiling. "And you wonder why I have issues committing."

Priest cleared his throat. "That's not—"

"It is," I interrupted. "I was stupid to ever let my emotions get involved. Especially after we'd agreed not to."

"Mal."

"Just go," I said. I hurt all over, ached in my body and in my heart, and having Priest sitting here pitying me was only making it worse.

He did as I asked. He stood up, muttered a goodbye, and slipped out the door.

As soon as I was alone in the room, I missed him. Part of me had wanted Priest to push back—to demand to stay and talk this through. To change his mind.

But he'd just left. And that was proof, definitive proof, that whatever we may have had before was over.

Chapter 24 - Priest

A month passed.

Mal had spent ten days recovering in the hospital—I received regular updates, as did the rest of the inner circle, from Dante at our church meetings. He'd been out of the hospital for two weeks now, and apparently, also according to Dante, he was recovering well. He wasn't going to be able to ride his bike anytime soon, nor was he going to have the same mobility in his shoulder that he'd had before the attack.

But that was a small price to pay for him being alive.

Not that I would know. Because the price I was paying was distance. I burned with shame when I thought about it, but I hadn't visited him at all since that first night in the hospital. And when he'd been released, he'd come to my cabin, knocked at the door and called my name.

I hadn't answered.

I knew it was cowardly. Worse than that—it was cruel. I'd barely given Mal an explanation. I'd told him we should be friends, and then I couldn't even bring myself to visit him as a friend. Because I knew he'd demand a conversation— he *deserved* one—and I didn't know how to have it. I didn't know what to say.

All I knew was that I was fucking *terrified*.

I groaned, rolling over in bed and rubbing my palms hard against my eyes. Someone was pounding on my door repeatedly. "Priest!" Blade shouted. "I know you're in there! Open up!"

I grabbed my phone. God, it was late—nearly ten in the morning. I never stayed in bed this late.

"Coming," I said, then tugged on sweatpants and stumbled down the stairs.

I opened the door and Blade pushed past me, laden down with big lattes and baked goods from Stella's. "Jeez, Priest. Still in bed at this hour?"

"I know," I said, then rubbed my hand over my hair. "Haven't been sleeping well."

Blade paused, then slid one of the lattes toward me and unpacked the croissants. They smelled amazing, but I found I wasn't hungry. The coffee called me, though, and I took a grateful sip.

"Not sleeping?" Blade asked. "What's going on?"

"Just bad dreams," I said. "Seems like I can't get a full night's sleep since that night."

Blade nodded. "What are the dreams?"

The worst part of the dreams was that they weren't anything special. My brain just replayed the events of that night—the crack of the gunshot, the weight of Mal's body collapsed against mine, the sticky heat of the blood gushing under my palm, pulsing out with each beat of his heart.

"There was just so much blood," I said. It's not that I hadn't seen injuries like that before—hell, I'd seen worse. But it was so unexpected, and so close, and I'd been *so* sure that I was losing Mal. With every fresh pulse of blood and every wet choking breath, I'd felt him slipping away. "I keep having the same dream. It's the same as it was that night, except—except Mal doesn't make it."

Blade sighed. "Talking to him might help that, you know. He's alive. He's walking around. He *misses* you."

I cringed. "I will, it's just…"

"Just what?" Blade asked. He crossed his arms over his chest, pinning me with his serious gaze.

I realized then he hadn't shown up with coffee and pastries just to be nice—he was sick of me hiding out. And it was his presidential duty to get to the bottom of whatever was going on between Mal and me. I rubbed the back of my neck, exhausted and ashamed. I was Blade's vice, and his mentor, and I'd put him in a real shitty position acting like this.

"Mal made it this time," I said. "But what about next time?"

"What do you mean, *next time*?" Blade asked. "Xavier's dead. There's not going to *be* a next time. You made sure of that."

"No, I mean…" I took a sip of my coffee and tried to get my thoughts straight. I hadn't voiced these fears before, and saying them out loud made me feel too vulnerable. "This is a dangerous life, Blade, you know that."

Blade nodded. "Just as well as you do. And Mal knows it, too."

I sighed. "Every time we think we've finally settled things down, some new risk and danger pops up. There's never going to be a time where there's *not* violence. Risk. It's just the way of things. I knew that when I founded this club, but it's... it's more real now. The risks are *greater*."

Blade didn't interject. He just watched me thoughtfully, hands wrapped around his coffee cup.

"I can't go through it again," I said quietly. Even just the hypothetical made my heart crawl into my throat. "I can't lose another man I love. I can't do it. It'd break me. This was already too close of a call—I'm too close to Mal. If I want the club to survive, and if *I'm* going to survive, I need to put some distance between us."

"Priest," Blade said softly.

"That way, if, God forbid, something happens, I won't be— won't be *ruined*. It'd be hard, but I'd survive."

I nodded to myself. This was the right decision. Even if it was challenging in the short-term, it'd be better for the club. And for me.

"You know that's not the right call," Blade said.

I paused. "What?"

"Come on," Blade said. "If one of the members came to you talking this nonsense, you'd slap them upside the head."

Well—even if that was true, this was a different situation. Wasn't it? I sipped my coffee, brow furrowed.

"I almost lost Logan," Blade said.

I started, then looked up and met Blade's eyes. His dark eyes were warm with concern, and I suddenly noticed the crow's feet at the corners, and the laugh lines near his mouth. Blade was a good president, I'd never doubted that. But I did sometimes still think of him as the young, bright-eyed prospect who'd joined all those years ago. He'd been through just as much as all of us, though—and he knew the fear of loss, same as I did. He'd lost Ankh, too.

"It would've been easier to run away," Blade said. "To push Logan away and go back to the way things were. But I would've been lying to myself. Acting like a coward. Ankh taught me that this club was supposed to be a place where we could build a home. Be our real selves. A port in a storm. And how could I lead a club with that ethos if I was too afraid to follow my heart?" He grinned. "And, obviously, it paid off for me."

"When'd you get so wise?" I deflected, as I turned over Blade's words in my mind.

"Good leadership growing up," he said. "Seriously. If you love Mal—really love him—then the last thing you need to do is run from that. That'll destroy you sooner than some imagined what-if."

"It's not that simple," I said. "If something goes wrong, it puts the whole club at risk. Not just—not just loss, but even something as simple as breaking up. It affects all of us."

"Of course it does," Blade said. "We all want you two to be happy. Haven't you noticed what's happened to the club lately?"

"What do you mean?" I asked, tilting my head to the side. Suddenly confused. Had something changed that I didn't notice?

"We're stable," Blade said. "The club's foundation is strong. Especially now that we have the two chapters—if something happened between you and Mal, and you needed time apart, or even time away from the club, you could do that. And the club would be fine. It's strong." He stepped closer and put his hand on my shoulder. "You built something lasting. You're safe to take these risks here."

My heart twisted. Blade was right—Ankh and I had built a strong club. With a strong foundation.

And... maybe I didn't need to worry about turning the club on its axis if something went wrong between Mal and me. But that didn't mean I could just jump into a relationship. Not when...

I looked over Blade's shoulder at the fridge, where the photo of Ankh and me was in the center, arms swung around each other, smiling wide.

"I don't know what's worse," I murmured. "The fear of losing another man I love—or loving someone new in the first place."

Blade followed my line of sight to the photo. He hummed in understanding. "Is that what's been holding you back? This whole time?"

I was so tired. Tired of trying to change my feelings, trying to hide, trying to grapple with the loss of my husband and my new feelings for my oldest friend.

"Of course," I said. "I thought I'd never want to be with anyone again. I was okay with that. Falling for Mal has made me reframe what I thought the rest of my life would look like." I met his eyes. "I'm not getting any younger."

"And that's exactly why you *shouldn't* run from this," Blade said seriously. "Ankh would want you to be happy. He would want you to live a full life—he wouldn't want you to beat yourself up over your capacity to love. Your feelings for Mal don't mean you loved Ankh any *less.* It's a testament to how much love you have to give."

I'd never thought about it that way.

"Oh," I said quietly, still gazing at the photo.

Loving Mal didn't mean I didn't love Ankh. It wasn't a competition. And the relationships weren't the same— they didn't need to be. This was just a different chapter in my life. It didn't mean I would forget Ankh, and it didn't diminish what we'd had.

Blade was right. Ankh would want me to take risks to be happy. He would want me to live. And I hadn't been, not fully.

"And honestly, if you were going to fall for someone, you know Ankh would be happy it's Mal," Blade said with a grin. "He's a great president—and he's been family to this club for as long as it's existed. And you know Ankh thought he was hot."

I barked a surprised laugh. "You're right about that. It used to irritate me how much he'd talk about Mal's ass."

"See? I don't think you could do much better than Mal." Blade squeezed my shoulder, then pulled me into a rough hug. "So don't beat yourself up over it, okay? And please talk to Mal. He's climbing the walls."

"All right, all right," I said, muffled into Blade's shoulder. "I'll talk to him."

"Good," Blade said, pulling away with a broad grin. He gathered his coffee, left the pastries with me, and headed toward the door.

"Hey, Blade?" I said.

He glanced over his shoulder. "Yeah?"

"Thanks," I said. "For stopping by."

"Of course," Blade said with an inquisitive tilt of his head. "You'd do it for any of us."

He left me alone in the kitchen, with the pastries waiting for me and a lot on my mind. With a sigh, I moved to the couch and dropped into the center of it, coffee in hand. I gazed up at the photo of Ankh on the mantle—the same one I'd seen Mal looking at the first night I'd brought him here.

"This is so fucking hard," I sighed to the photo. "I miss you so much. I wish there was just a sign. A way to know I was heading down the right path."

I sighed and leaned heavily back into the couch, tipping my head back.

My phone buzzed in my pocket. I fished it out, expecting a message from Blade or Dante—but it was a call. A call from Mal.

His smiling face on the caller ID screen made my heart do a somersault in my chest.

I shook my head in disbelief, then glanced at the photo. "You're right. It's time for me to stop being a coward."

A phone call wouldn't do it, though. Mal deserved better than that. I needed to apologize. I needed to see him face to face.

I could only hope that he'd still be willing to listen to me.

Chapter 25 - Mal

"Come on," Nix urged. He set the book he'd brought me—one of his beloved sci-fi novels—on my coffee table, and then sat next to me on my couch. "At least come hang out downstairs. You've got to stop wallowing up here all alone."

"I'm not wallowing," I said as I sank a little deeper into the couch.

I knew he was right, though. My studio used to be a refuge for me—a place of peace. But now, after four weeks, it was beginning to feel a little like a cell. I'd been relieved to get out of the hospital, but I'd had to continue my slow recovery at home. And even when I was feeling good, I found I wasn't up to hanging out with the guys in the clubhouse.

Because one person hadn't showed.

Priest hadn't visited me in the hospital or the clubhouse. He hadn't texted. Hadn't answered any of my calls.

Had he even asked about me?

"I'm just tired," I said.

"We both know that's not it," Nix said gently. "Talk to me."

I rubbed my hand over my forehead. Both Dante and Tru had been bugging me about Priest, ever since the day two weeks ago when I'd made my way to his cabin, only to be met with silence, despite the fact his bike was parked out front. I didn't want to make either of my kids worry about me even more, though, so I'd tried to deflect their concerns.

"I just miss him," I admitted. "In the hospital, he told me we should go back to being friends."

Nix nodded and placed a gentle hand on my knee, silently encouraging me to continue.

"But this isn't even *friendship*," I said. "I haven't seen him at all in these past four weeks. It'd be easier to handle the shift back into being just friends if he was acting like a friend at all."

"He probably just needs some time to adjust, too," Nix said.

"I know," I said. "I got *shot*, though. He should adjust faster."

Nix laughed, surprised. "Honestly, that's a good point."

I shook my head. "I just feel stupid. I'd made it so clear that I wasn't going to let my heart get involved. I can't even be angry that he wants to go back to how things were before. It was too good to be true." My heart twisted at the memory of our last night together. "I just...didn't know a relationship could be like that. Where someone could be your best friend and *also* your partner. But, of course, Priest knew that."

"You think it's Ankh's memory holding him back?" Nix asked.

"Of course," I said, even as my stomach turned admitting it. "And it's not 'holding him back.' He's just—making the right decision. I was stupid to think we could have a real relationship—why would he want that with me after what he'd had with Ankh? Whatever we had, it can't compare to that. I'm just the runner-up." I cringed, turning away from Nix and his carefully soft gaze. "I'm the consolation prize. Of course he doesn't want me. We're better off as friends, anyway."

"That's not true at all," a familiar, warm voice said from the doorway.

I started, looking up wide-eyed.

Priest stood in the doorway, in jeans and a soft flannel, hands tucked into his pockets. With his shoulders rolled forward and a concerned expression on his face, he looked almost... shy. Nervous. My heart hammered in my chest, and conflicting emotions flooded me: relief that he was here, anger that it'd taken so long, embarrassment that he'd heard me pour my heart out to Nix.

"I was going to say something about your interpretation," Nix said, then cast a serious look to Priest, "but it seems like I don't have to."

He patted my knee, then stood to leave. Nix pinned Priest with another hard look as he slipped by him in the doorway, and to my shock, Priest looked a little ashamed.

Priest closed the door to my apartment behind him, and then we were alone.

I sighed and crossed my arms over my chest. Despite my anger, something slotted into place at the sight of Priest standing in my apartment after all this time. My studio had felt so empty these past weeks. Like I'd been waiting for him.

"Can I sit down?" Priest asked.

A small, snide, immature part of me wanted to say no. To turn him away, kick him out, make him hurt the way I'd hurt when he'd left me alone in the hospital. But we were both grown men, and I was too old to waste more time with pettiness like that.

"You going to explain yourself?" I asked.

"If you'll let me," Priest said gently.

"Then sit down," I said, nodding at the place on the couch Nix had vacated.

Priest sat close to me on the couch and gently took my hand in his. The contact felt so good—so *right*—and I closed my eyes, bracing myself to be rejected again. Surely, he'd come to smooth things over so we could go back to being *just friends*.

"I'm in love with you," Priest said.

The words stole my breath from my lungs. My heart hammered as I looked up and met his warm blue eyes. This sure as hell wasn't what I'd expected. I hadn't even dared to hope. "*What*?"

"I'm so sorry," Priest said. "You needed me these past few weeks. And I abandoned you."

"Yeah," I admitted. "You *did*. *Why*? I just—what do you mean you're in love with me?"

"Exactly what it sounds like," Priest said. He kept his hand folded over mine. "I was stupid—and cowardly. And I don't know if I can ever make that up to you. But after Xavier shot you..."

He closed his eyes and took a steadying breath.

"After he shot you, I really thought I lost you. You passed out in my arms, and the bleeding just wouldn't stop. There was nothing I could do. Even as the paramedics loaded you into the ambulance, I thought—I thought you were gone."

"You saved me, though," I said. "If you hadn't put pressure on it, I would've been gone."

Priest cringed. "I hate to think about that. What would've happened if I hadn't followed you?"

"So why didn't you come back to the hospital?" I asked. "Why'd you ignore me when I came to your door?"

"I'm not proud of that," Priest said. "In fact, I'm really fucking ashamed. But... all I could think about was how losing Ankh had almost killed me."

I nodded. I remembered the weeks after Ankh's death—how Priest had been sequestered in the clubhouse, in bed nearly constantly, barely eating, pushing the members away when they'd tried to encourage him to come downstairs. His grief had been like a disease of its own, and he'd wasted away beneath it. It'd taken months for him to start to seem like himself again—and even after that, he was changed. Not a negative change, but certainly a different, more thoughtful, more present man.

"And I realized," Priest said, "that if I admitted to myself that I loved you, and if we were together—*really* together—that came with the risk of losing you. And that scared me so badly I just ran in the other direction."

"You had already been thinking about it, before I got shot?" I asked. "I thought—I thought you weren't interested in a relationship."

"I thought I wasn't either," Priest said. "At the beginning. But as soon as we got together, my feelings started to change." He laughed a little, shaking his head. "I've always been a romantic."

"You didn't say anything," I said.

"I felt guilty," Priest said. "Like I shouldn't have feelings for anyone else, not after losing my husband."

"I didn't want to pressure you," I said. "I wanted you to feel safe with me—didn't want you think I was trying to take Ankh's place. I'm still not. I know our relationship is different."

"It is different," Priest agreed with a nod. "But that doesn't make it any less real. Or any less meaningful. And I want... I want us to be together. I want you to be mine. And I want to be *yours*."

I exhaled hard. "I gotta admit, this wasn't what I was expecting from this conversation."

"I know I've been a jackass," Priest said.

"Yeah. I get it, though," I said.

And I did, honestly—I'd never considered what witnessing my near-death might have done to Priest. I was focused on my own recovery, but now that Priest had told me, I understood that he'd been traumatized by the shooting, as well. It'd made the pain of losing Ankh resurface in a very tangible way. No wonder he'd hidden himself away.

"You didn't want to feel that pain again," I said.

"I still don't," Priest said. "Losing Ankh was so painful, I didn't think I'd ever be able to love someone again. But… life is funny that way." He met my gaze, serious and soft. "I've been blessed twice. And I'm not going to throw that way just because I'm afraid of losing you. Ankh would be so embarrassed of me if I did that."

"You think so?" I asked. Did he really think Ankh would approve? Did he really want to pursue a relationship with me? I was reeling. I scooted a little closer and pressed our thighs together, hungry for Priest's touch.

"I know so," Priest said. "And I'm so fucking sorry I abandoned you these past few weeks."

"You should be," I teased. "I've been lonely."

Priest looked briefly devastated. "I've really had my head up my ass. Blade talked some sense into me."

"That sounds about right," I said.

Priest still looked unsure, so I leaned forward and kissed him gently.

"I love you, too," I murmured against his lips. "I already told you that."

"I know," Priest said. "But I wouldn't be surprised if the last few weeks made you change your mind."

"Gonna take more than that to drive me away," I said.

The tight line of Priest's shoulders eased a little as he kissed me again. He pulled his hand from mine, but only to set both at my waist instead, rubbing gentle circles there as he kissed me slowly and tenderly.

He pulled away and touched my cheek softly, and I turned my head into his touch gently. "So I didn't turn you off of the commitment thing entirely?" he asked.

I remembered what I'd said in the hospital and winced. It'd been an emotional reaction, but I didn't have any desire to take it back. I still meant what I'd said.

"It reminded me of Melanie," I said. "She's the only person I've really loved—other than you. And when she left me, she didn't just break my heart. She broke my ability to trust. I'd been so busy raising Dante that I didn't bother to let my heart heal. I just let it callus over. It was easier to give up on relationships than to risk getting abandoned again." I sighed. "But…a near-death experience can act as a wake-up call. Thirty years is a long time to waste licking that old wound."

"I don't think you wasted it at all," Priest said, brow furrowed. "You built a club. You raised your son into a good man. You've got a whole community of people who love you."

I paused. Maybe Priest was right. Maybe I'd needed those years to focus on myself, and my son, before I was ready to open my heart to someone else again. "I'd never met someone who made me want to try, anyway."

"Until now?" Priest asked, with a small, teasing smile.

"Yeah," I said. "Until now. Something about all those years of friendship made it pretty easy to fall for you. And I'm finally ready, I think." I paused and grinned. "Unless we're too old to give it a shot."

Priest scoffed and rolled his eyes dramatically. His grip tightened on my waist, but it was still gentle, mindful of my still-healing injury.

"No way," he said. "I think we can give the young bucks in our club a run for their money."

"Think so?" I asked. I gripped his thigh, just above his knee, and then slid my hand up his inner thigh, following the seam of his jeans. I let my hand linger just inches away from his groin. I was nearly dizzy with relief, with desire— he *wanted* me. He wanted *us.* And it was so easy, and natural, to slide back into our sexy, playful dynamic, built on decades of trust and friendship. "Think you can prove it?"

His blue eyes sparkled. "Yeah, I think so," he said, then pulled me in for a hard kiss.

*

PRIEST

The pressure of Mal's hand on my inner thigh was like a brand, sending a hot rush of arousal through me. Fuck, I wanted him so badly. The weeks without him had only made me want him more—only made me realize how well we fit together, how our bodies worked together like two pieces of a puzzle. I ached for his touch, his kiss, his hands on me. Now that we were together, I never wanted to let him go.

Mal stood up, took my hand, and guided me to the bed. I lay down on top of the covers and watched him carefully as he moved to join me, my attention focused on his shoulder, and the way he still held it slightly stiff.

"We don't have to do anything," I said. "You're still healing."

"Yeah," he said. "I'm healing well. And I want you."

"I want you, too," I said. "So fucking badly. Come here."

Mal straddled me, his thighs straddling my hips, and leaned down to kiss me deeply. The kiss was slow, lazy, but intense—his tongue slid against mine, his teeth set into my lower lip, promising more. Still, I was careful with my touch. No matter how badly I wanted him, I wasn't going to hurt him more. Not after everything he'd been through. I slipped my hands under the hem of his shirt and skated them gently over his lower back, soothingly.

"I'm not going to break," Mal said with a small smile. "You want to see it? Make you feel better?"

My heart flipped in my chest. Strangely enough... I did think it would make me feel better to see with my own eyes that he was healing up. To know that yes, he'd been shot. He'd bled out in my arms. That had happened... and we'd both survived. He was recovering. Maybe seeing that with my own eyes would stop the dreams.

"Yeah," I said. "Please, let me." I gently curled my fingers in the hem of his shirt and tugged it over his head.

Mal climbed off me and spread out on his stomach on the mattress, head pillowed on one arm. I lay on my side next to him, still dressed, and ran hand down the divot of his spine.

His shoulder was bandaged tightly, white gauze taped down across the wound, but it was clean. There was no blood visible, *nothing* visible through the gauze. His dark skin was bruised, though, mottled purple across his deltoid and down his back. I traced my fingers over the edge of the bruises, then the edge of the tape.

"Does it hurt?" I asked. Even though I knew the answer, I wanted to hear him talk about it—wanted to know everything I'd been stupid enough to miss.

"Yeah," Mal said. "It hurts like a bitch. It was worse before, though. I can finally sleep through the night now. And shower, that's a goddamn blessing. Dante's been helping me change the dressing."

"I can help do that now," I said. I leaned down to press a kiss to the top of his shoulder, above the gauze. "If you'll let me."

"I don't know," Mal said. "It's pretty nasty."

"I've been in a motorcycle club for nearly four decades," I said with a laugh. "You think I can't handle a mostly healed gunshot wound?"

"Good point," Mal said. "It's not nearly as gross as road rash."

"Ugh," I said. "Don't make me think about road rash right now."

Mal quirked an eyebrow at me. "What do you want to think about instead?"

I could've said something snarky and horny, gotten back to kissing him, but something in my chest still ached at the sight of the wound. Especially knowing he'd handled the worst of the healing alone.

"You were there for me through the worst of my grief," I said gently, still leaning over him with my lips close to his shoulder. "When I could hardly get out of bed, when I couldn't sleep, when I could hardly imagine continuing on… you were there for me even when I wouldn't let you be. I don't know if I ever thanked you for that."

"You don't have to thank me," Mal said softly. "You would've done it for me, too."

"I like to think I would've," I admitted. "But I haven't been here for you so far."

"You are now," Mal said. "That's what matters."

How could he be so kind? So forgiving? I wasn't sure what I'd done to deserve this—to not only have one great love of my life, but two. And to have Mal understand why I'd ran, and to forgive me so easily. I wasn't going to abandon him again. The fear of loss was still there, but it was clearly worth it now—worth having Mal next to me.

"I am," I said. "And I'm not going anywhere."

"Good," Mal said, and then that coy smirk was on his lips again. "Now stop treating me like I'm fragile." He reached out and hooked two fingers in my waistband. "Get these off. I missed you."

I hopped off the bed, tugged my shirt overhead, and then shucked my jeans off quickly as well. Mal rolled gingerly onto his back, watching me with his eyes dark with interest. He was so gorgeous—his broad, muscular chest, the wiry gray hair dusting his chest, his strong core shifting with each breath. His hands went to his waistband, about to pop the button on his jeans.

"Quit that," I said, then raised my eyebrows. "I want to be the one to do that."

"Oh, I see," Mal said teasingly.

So instead of popping his jeans open, he simply spread his legs a little wider and ran his palm over the swell of his cock trapped in his jeans. Fuck, that was hot. I stood pinned to the spot for a moment, watching him rub his hand up and down as he watched me. My own cock twitched in interest, hardening in my shorts. Mal's gaze zeroed in on it, and his lips parted.

"Get over here," he said. "Fuck, you're sexy. Get these off me before I do it myself."

"Demanding," I said with a grin. I knelt on the bed between his spread legs, then leaned down to mouth a kiss at his sternum as I skated my hand down his torso to the waistband of his jeans.

"It's been a while," Mal grumbled, and well, he had a point there. I dragged my mouth across the muscle of his pec, then pressed the flat of my tongue to his peaked nipple, savoring the low groan that pulled from his chest. Then I popped the button on his jeans and sat up just enough to tug them off his body.

Then he was spread out in front of me, his thick muscular legs, the curve of his bicep with his good arm propping his head up, and the thick line of his cock visible through his tight underwear. I took a moment to savor the sight, drinking him in, from his narrow ankles all the way to his smirking face and the deep crow's feet at the corners of his warm eyes.

"God, you're sexy," I murmured.

"You're not so bad yourself," Mal said with his eyebrow raised. "Now *please* get up here and fuck me."

"Well, when you ask so nicely," I said. Then I climbed onto the bed next to him and maneuvered him so we were face to face, ensuring Mal was on his good side. "You want me to fuck you?"

"You want me to say it again?" Mal asked, then leaned forward and kissed me.

"Love hearing you say it," I said. "Can you blame me?"

We traded slow, thorough kisses. I pulled away only long enough to grab the lube, and then tugged Mal closer, so we were tangled together. I ran my palm up and down his thigh, then over his hip to his ass, squeezing hard.

"Get a move on," Mal said, smiling into the kiss. He nipped at my lower lip in punctuation. "Please, Priest, fuck me."

I wanted to take my time—wanted to be careful—but I also didn't want to make Mal wait any longer than he already had. I wasn't in the mood to tease him, or even draw things out, not right now. I wanted him to feel good—wanted to show him with my hands and my mouth that I was here for him. Right now, and for the rest of our lives, too.

We hurried out of our underwear, and I only had a moment to admire the gorgeous curve of his cock before we were pressed back together. I stretched him open on my fingers as I kissed him, working two in slowly, and my cock throbbed with every little sound my fingers wrung from Mal's chest. I thrust my fingers in and out, so slowly it made Mal sigh and moan into my mouth. He hooked his leg a little higher onto my hip, then carded one hand through my hair.

Soon I had three fingers in him, thrusting in and out deep and slow, as Mal rocked his hips back to meet my touch. "You tease," he said.

"Not teasing," I said. "Just enjoying." I crooked my fingers just so, finding that place inside him that made him shiver and gasp into my mouth. His hips bucked back like he couldn't control it, like his body was begging for more.

Mal reached back and grabbed my wrist. "My turn to enjoy," he murmured.

Then with a smirk, he pushed at my shoulder, guiding me suddenly flat on my back. I huffed an exhale in surprise. Mal straddled my hips, then reached over to the nightstand to dig a condom out of the drawer—I took the opportunity to run my hands adoringly up his sides, then his arms, then the nape of his neck. Mal leaned down and kissed me hot and dirty on the mouth, fucking his tongue inside, taking control. God, that turned me on—even more so when he sat up, then moved down so he was straddling my thighs. He shot me a smirk, then rolled the condom on me with practiced ease.

I groaned at the sensation of his hand on my cock, even so briefly it was like a shockwave rattling through me. I tossed my head back against the pillow, arching toward his touch.

"Wow," Mal said with a smile. He squeezed the base of my cock and I gasped.

"Fuck, Mal, now who's teasing?" I asked, reaching to skim my hand across his hip.

"You're right," he said. "God, I missed you. Thought about this so much the last few weeks."

"I did too," I admitted. "Want you so bad."

"You have me," Mal said. Then he shifted up again, straddling my hips, and got his hand slick with lube. Then he pressed his hips back, guiding my cock so it was nestled between his muscular ass cheeks—not slipping inside, just rutting in between. Mal groaned like it was the best thing he'd ever felt.

"You're so big," he groaned. "Feels so hot."

"Fuck," I groaned. I slid my hands up his thighs, to his hips, and then rocked up, fucking my cock between his cheeks.

"Yeah," Mal said. "Fuck, missed you."

I couldn't really form sentences, not when Mal was so gorgeous and strong above me, his head tipped back in pleasure. Then he reached back, gripped the base of my cock, and guided it until the head of my cock was pressed right against his hole.

Then, without any teasing, he rocked his hips back, and sank down onto my cock.

I groaned low and loud. He was so fucking tight, and he took me slowly but steadily, surrounding me in that slick heat until his ass was flush against my hips. I gasped, struggling to stay still as he adjusted to the sensation of my cock so deep inside him. I kept one hand at his hip, and I skated my other around to wrap around his cock and jerk him steadily.

He moaned my name. Then he leaned forward, planted one hand on my chest, and began to rock his hips on my cock.

He rolled his hips, lifting up and down on my cock. I planted my feet on the mattress and matched his pace, careful not to drive too hard into him—still mindful of his injury. Instead, we found a rhythm that was slow and deep, so my cock dragged inside him in a way that made him shiver and shake, and the tight slick heat of his body made me dizzy with pleasure.

"Gonna come," Mal managed to say around a moan. His mouth was slack, brow furrowed in gorgeous pleasure.

I tightened my grip on his cock and tried to fuck my cock impossibly deeper into his body. "Come on," I encouraged. "Come on my cock, baby."

Mal shoved his hips back hard, taking me so deep I gasped as my own pleasure swirled hot and overwhelming inside me. "You too," he said. "Come with me."

I gasped—it was like his words alone dragged me close to the edge. Mal collapsed so we were chest to chest, and I barely managed to keep my hand around his cock where it was pinned between us. I fucked into him, the motion rocking him forward so his cock rutted into my fist. Our lips met in a sloppy kiss—less a kiss and more an open-mouthed panting against each other—as my pleasure curled hotter and more urgent inside me.

Then, Mal gasped against my mouth and came hard; his hot release coated my hand and my chest, making a mess between us. As he came, he shivered and clenched around me, becoming somehow even tighter. It was all so much— the tight heat, the gorgeous sounds he made, and knowing that I was the one who made him feel that good. And who would get to make him feel this good forever.

The heat inside me coiled tight and then released, and I thrust deep inside him as my orgasm rocked me to my core. Pleasure flooded me from deep in my hips, rushing across my skin all the way to my fingertips and I cried out Mal's name as I came.

It seemed to last forever, waves of pleasure washing over me as Mal and I caught our breath together.

With a sigh, Mal shifted just enough for me to pull out, but thankfully, he didn't go anywhere. He just lay flat on top of me, his face pressed into the crook of my neck. I didn't even care about the sticky mess between us. My joy and relief at having him close overwhelmed everything else.

"Mm," Mal murmured.

I wrapped my arms around his waist, hugging him close to me, and kissed wherever I could reach on his face: his temple, forehead, the bridge of his nose. "Hmm what?"

His smile curved against my skin. "I love you."

My heart flipped. "I love you, too."

The words rolled off my tongue like they'd been there, waiting, since the first time we kissed. I knew all the way into the deepest parts of myself that I was never going to let him go.

Chapter 26 - Mal

"Wow," I said dreamily, as I ran my hand down the muscled plane of Priest's chest. "I need a shower. And maybe a nap."

"We just woke up," Priest said with a laugh. "You can't need a nap yet."

Sure, we'd woken up a little under an hour ago, but we'd spent that time having some athletic morning sex. My shoulder was finally healed enough that Priest didn't feel like he needed to be extra careful, and we were more than enjoying our return to the rough, animalistic sex we both adored. It'd been a month since Priest and I had gotten our act together, and we were done wasting time. I didn't officially live in his cabin, but it was close. My clothes were mixed into his laundry, my toothbrush on his countertop— and his things were dotted in my studio apartment, too. We spent every night together.

Life was good.

Better than good. Life was perfect. Better than I'd ever imagined it could be.

"So what?" I asked, stretching long in his bed. "Why not take a nap at nine in the morning? We're not busy today."

"Gotta get our act together for the barbeque this afternoon," Priest said. "I'm on grill duty."

"Don't say that like you don't demand to be on grill duty every time." I poked him in the ribs, and Priest squawked and rolled away. "You'd pitch a fit if anyone else touched your beloved grill."

"All right, maybe that's true," Priest said with a grin. "What can I say? I simply want the best for our club. And the food's the best when I grill it."

"They're lucky to have you," I said. "So thoughtful."

Priest tugged me into his arms. "*I'm* lucky to have *them*," he said. "And you."

My heart swelled as Priest drew me into a lazy, languid kiss. "You're so sentimental," I murmured.

"Can't help it," Priest said, smiling against my mouth. "Guess love makes me cheesy."

"It's rubbing off on me." I kissed him again. "I love *you*. I think *I'm* the lucky one."

The kiss deepened, and I ran my hands over the curve of Priest's pecs, then his abs, then his hips. His body was so well-known to me now, and the familiarity only made it better. I knew his body nearly as well as my own now, and I was getting really, really good at slowly bringing him to orgasm. I loved driving him crazy. Maybe the shower and the nap could wait—round two was sounding more appealing.

Just as I was sliding my hand over Priest's hip to grab his ass, moaning as his tongue dipped into my mouth, we were interrupted by someone knocking noisily at the front door to the cabin.

"Hey!" Tru called. "Put your pants on! Open up!"

"You heard the man!" Dante shouted.

"Come on!" Blade yelled. "We're on a schedule here!"

More laughter, more voices. It sounded like half the club was outside. Laughing, I kissed Priest again, sweeter this time.

"This is the downside of having dozens of children," I said. "Can't get a moment alone."

"Well, I'll make them regret that," Priest said with a grin as he levered off the bed, gorgeously naked, and padded down the stairs. I leaned up against the headboard, laughing incredulously as Priest shouted, "All right, all right, hold on, you animals."

The door swung open, and then there was a chorus of screeches and shouts. ("Augh, come on!" "No! I wasn't ready!" "Put some pants on!")

Priest laughed uproariously. "That's what you get for showing up here this early!"

"Jeez!" Blade said. "At least hold a pillow or something!"

"What do you want?" Priest asked, still laughing. "It's a little early to start getting ready for the barbeque, isn't it?"

"We're all hanging out and getting ready," Blade said. "Come on, come to the clubhouse so you can make the barbeque rub the way you like it, or else Logan is going to do it."

"Oh, shit," Priest said. "I can't have anyone messing with my rub."

"Thought so," Blade grumbled.

"We'll see you in a bit," Priest said.

I heard him make him way up the stairs, and Tru shouted, "Not an ass shot, too!"

Priest reappeared in the doorway, grinning mischievously. "They'll think twice before showing up unannounced from now on, I think."

"Good work, vice," I said through my laughter. I motioned for him to step closer, then set my hand as his hip as he leaned over the bed to kiss me. "Guess round two will have to wait until later today."

"I'm not in any rush," Priest murmured.

No need to hurry, because we had all the time in the world. We exchanged a few more lazy, easy kisses, and then finally climbed out of bed to get dressed. I tugged my club leather on over my shirt and turned toward the bedroom door.

"Wait a second," Priest said.

"What?" I asked, glancing over my shoulder.

He stepped closer, and I turned to face him, smiling. Priest smoothed his hands down my chest, straightening out the lapels of my jacket.

"Nothing. Just like seeing you in the leather." He shot me a sly wink. "Like getting you out of it even more."

"We'll do that later," I promised, then tugged him in for a kiss.

We walked the short path between the cabin and the clubhouse, our fingers loosely tangled together as we strolled. It was mid-morning, but the clubhouse was already noisy with activity: laughter rang from the backyard, and the doors were flung open to let in the cool air. Barbeques like this one were an all-day affair, and I couldn't wait to spend the day idling by the bonfire and helping prep huge amounts of food in the gorgeous kitchen.

As soon as we stepped over the threshold, a chorus of shouts greeted us.

"There they are!" Dante yelled over the din. "Nice of you to finally join us, Dad!"

He had a pan of muffins fresh from the oven in hand; he set them on the stove, then dusted an excess bit of flour from his forefinger into Heath's nose. Heath rolled his eyes fondly, then leaned over the muffins to savor the sweet, wafting scent.

"There's coffee," Raven said, closing his laptop and hopping off the couch. "Need some?"

"Oh, I do," Gunnar said. He caught Raven's wrist and tugged him down for a quick kiss. Raven laughed, then took his empty mug—good thing we had an industrial-sized coffeemaker.

"Hey, you're here!" Joker called as he thundered down the stairs with Brennan behind him. "Heard you gave Blade an eyeful this morning. Is this a career pivot to stripping?"

Brennan barked a laugh. "Honestly, if this club got into stripping, I think you could make a lot of money. Maybe this year's Halloween fundraiser?" He followed Joker into the kitchen with his hands set at Joker's hips possessively.

Raven handed Priest and me our coffees. Priest ruffled Raven's hair affectionately, and Raven ducked his chin and brushed Priest's hand away. But I could tell he liked it. My heart flipped with fondness at the gesture.

"No, I think he's onto something," Tru said.

He was sprawled in Priest's preferred armchair, sitting in it all wrong—his legs over one armrest, his back leaning against the other, head tipped back so he could see into the kitchen. Beau snuck into the kitchen and grabbed two muffins from Heath, then leaned over the back of the chair to hand one to Tru.

"Thanks, babe," Tru said. "Read my mind. Anyway, Tex, if you did your whole cowboy thing but in a stripping capacity at Ballast, we could seriously get some cash collected for the hospital. Oh! And Beau could get the firefighters involved!"

"You clearly haven't seen the guys I work with," Beau said, laughing.

"It's for a good cause," Tru pouted.

Tex adjusted his Stetson on his head and stroked his red beard thoughtfully. "Well, if it's for a good cause..."

Jazz squawked and threw an arm around Tex's shoulders. "*My* Tex? Considering stripping? Are pigs flying?"

Tex blushed. "Just considering. Come on, let's see how the grill is heating up."

"You already got the grill started?" Priest asked. "Without me?"

"You were taking too long," Jazz said with a grin. "Don't worry, you're still the boss around here."

Priest grinned at me, then took my hand and guided me outside, following Tex and Jazz. The backyard was buzzing with energy, too—Siren, Star, and Eli were setting up the volleyball net, laughing as Gretel bounded between them nipping at their heels and generally getting in the way.

"Gretel, leave them alone!" Rebel called. He snapped his fingers at Gretel, and she yipped happily and bounded over to where he was lounging in a camp chair near the crackling firepit. Coop intercepted the dog, though, scooping her into his arms. She wriggled, tail wagging so hard it made her entire butt move as she licked at Coop's chin.

"Aw, come on," Rebel said. "Don't let her do that."

"Like you don't," Coop teased. He put Gretel down, then leaned down and kissed Rebel, dog kisses be damned.

"Ah, the grillmaster is here," Nix said with a grin. He clapped Priest on the shoulder, and then did the same to me, too. "Glad you two could finally make it."

Dawson sidled up and wound his arm around Nix's waist. "How's that cabin treating you?" he asked, then winked.

"Gotta say," Priest said, tugging me close, "I'm pretty happy for the extra space these days."

"I am too," I said with a grin. "Nice to be able to make some noise."

"Like that stops you in the Crew Motel," Nix said with a smirk. "Now come on, Dawson, I have to put my casserole in the oven."

Nix and Dawson walked almost directly into Maverick as he was stepping out of the clubhouse onto the porch. "Hey, guys," Maverick said. "Where's Gretel? Someone's been requesting her all morning."

Jonah followed behind, with Grace squirming and laughing in his arms. Jonah walked down the stairs and set Grace on her feet in the grass. She took a few steps, and as soon as Gretel saw her, the dog yipped gleefully and bounded over. She skidded a stop in front of Grace, then lowered her head to the ground, butt in the air, tail wagging and ready to play.

"We might have to get Gracie a dog of her own soon," Jonah said, then tugged Maverick in for a brief little kiss.

"She might have a sibling on the way, with the way Raven and Gunnar have been talking," Priest said.

"I keep hearing whispers of that," Jonah said. "I sure hope so."

Blade stuck his head out of the back door and glanced around. "All right, everyone get back in here for a quick toast!"

We filed back inside, laughing and knocking our shoulders into each other. Siren and Star were last, each of them holding one of Grace's hands as she toddled into the clubhouse.

"Everyone's here, right?" Blade asked, glancing around. The clubhouse was full of members, standing in the kitchen and lounging in the living room, and my heart swelled at the sight of it. I was so lucky to be here—to be in this room, with the man I loved, and to be able to call these people my family. I hooked my arm around Priest's waist and held him close, then dropped a quick kiss onto his cheek.

After a chorus of confirming shouts, Blade climbed onto a chair. Logan winced, looking a little nervous, and kept his hand on Blade's thigh like that could stop him from falling.

"Well, guys," Blade said, gazing around the club with his coffee mug in hand. "You all know we've been through a lot these past few months. Hell, past few *years.* We've faced a lot of challenges, and a lot of dangers."

Nods and murmurs of agreement.

"But we've grown a lot, too," Blade said. He nodded a Dante, Tru, and Mal. "And we've added more people into the fold, people who I've grown to consider family."

Dawson, Beau, and Brennan all grinned.

"And I think we all know why we're all here," Blade said. "Why this club has made it through so much—why we've only grown stronger despite the bumps in the road. And that's the leadership."

He raised his coffee cup toward me and Priest.

I blinked, widening my eyes. "What?"

Priest huffed a laugh. "Come on, Blade."

"I'm serious!" Blade said around a grin. "You two are the backbone of the club—the heart of it." Cheers and whoops of agreement. "Without your guidance, and wisdom, and leadership, this club wouldn't be what it is today. And I think I speak for all of us when I say we're glad you found each other. You're the glue that holds the club together, and we're all grateful for it."

"Hell, yeah!" Coop shouted. "Go, dads!"

That sent the club members into peals of laughter. I was flushed with joy and warmth, and I knew from the wide smile on Priest's face and the shimmer in his eyes that he was, too. We locked eyes and he smiled, shaking his head like he couldn't quite believe it. And I felt the same.

How the hell did we get so lucky?

"To Mal and Priest!" Blade shouted.

"Hear, hear!" the club members shouted back, and everyone raised their coffee mugs (and a few mimosas) in cheers.

"Please get down now," Logan said to Blade. "You're too excited, you're going to break your leg."

"Am not," Blade said warmly. He hopped down from the chair, though, and pulled Logan in for a sweet, lingering kiss.

Then Priest ran his hand over my back, and I leaned into the touch. "To us," Priest said, low and private in my ear.

I raised my mug in agreement. "To us." Even in the noise of the clubhouse, with our family all around us—when Priest looked at me like that, I felt like I was the only man on Earth. "I love you."

He smiled, and his blue eyes sparkled with joy. "I love you, too."

I tugged him in for a soft kiss, and around us, the members hooted their approval. In response I only deepened the kiss, slipping my tongue into Priest's mouth, relishing the familiar shape of his smile against my lips.

We were together. And with the club around us, we were home.

Chapter 27 - Priest

I was having a wonderful dream. Ever since I'd started spending my nights with Mal, I'd only had good dreams—no more of the nightmares that had plagued me before.

But this was a better dream than most.

I knew it was a dream, somehow, even in the midst of it. Didn't make it any less nice. It was a gorgeous, warm summer day, with the sun shining bright overhead and not a cloud in the blue sky. I was stretched out on a blanket right at the edge of Elkin Lake, so I could dip my toes into the icy-cold, still blue water. A delightful contrast to the warmth of the day, just right at the edge of too hot. I leaned back on my elbows and tipped my head back, sunning like a lizard.

"There you are, Harry," a deep, familiar voice said. Happiness flooded me at the sound, and I sat up straight to peer over my shoulder at the source.

Ankh strolled down the path toward me with a broad smile on his face. He looked young and strong—like he'd looked when we were in the prime of our lives together, when the club was growing and we were settling into our roles as president and vice with a group of young bikers that looked to us for guidance. Lean build, thick, dark hair, and those deep blue eyes I'd always found myself getting lost in.

"I was looking for you," he said as he sat down on the blanket at my side.

"I haven't gone anywhere," I said. "Don't plan on leaving Elkin Lake anytime soon."

"Good," Ankh said. He smiled and took my hand in his. "I've been keeping an eye on things, you know."

"Oh, yeah?" I asked, unsurprised and grinning. Of course, he'd been looking out for us—I'd felt it so many times. "How's the club looking? Up to snuff?"

Ankh hummed faux-thoughtfully, and I swatted at his knee.

He tilted his head, then shot me a half-smile, an expression so beloved and familiar that my heart clenched in my chest.

"I'm so proud of all of you," Ankh said. "Blade's really stepped up as president—he's doing an incredible job. Brought down the Vipers *and* met the love of his life at the same time? Lucky guy. And our Coop got over his cop-hate because of Logan's brother? Unbelievable. Tex and Jazz got their heads out of their asses... Maverick got the family he always dreamed of... And our own prospect got Dante to settle down." Ankh shook his head fondly. "I can't believe it, honestly. And that's not even mentioning everything that's happened to bring Hell's Ankhor and the Liberty Crew together."

"And what about our son?" I asked. "What do you think about that?"

Ankh's hand tightened around my own. "Gunnar's so good for him."

"Raven looks so much like you," I said. "More and more, the older he gets. And he's so happy with Gunnar."

"They're going to have a kid of their own pretty soon," Ankh said. "I can feel it."

"Never thought I'd see the day," I said, then laughed. "Gunnar, tending to a baby. He sure does love Grace, though. It's going to be wonderful."

"Yeah," Ankh said softly. "It *is* going to be wonderful."

Under the warm summer sun it was easy to lean against Ankh, rest my head on his shoulder, and let him wrap his arm around me. "I miss you, Aaron. We all do. But I really, really miss you."

"I know," Ankh said. "I'm proud of you for keeping on living. You know that, right?"

My heart twisted. I'd hoped he was but hearing it in that warm voice soothed an ache inside me I hadn't realized was still there. "You are?"

"Mal was the man who encouraged me to get my act together and come back to you. Without him, I don't know what I would've done. I'm so grateful, though. In a way, he started our life together." Ankh turned and pressed a kiss to my forehead. "You two are good for each other. You'll take care of each other. To have that friendship become something more, when you both needed it most... It's such a blessing."

I leaned heavily against Ankh. "Life's easier with him at my side these days."

"You deserve that," Ankh said. "You deserve to keep loving. You have so much love to give."

Then Ankh placed his hand on my cheek and guided me in for a soft kiss. It stole my breath away, though it only lasted a moment. "Let me ask you something," Ankh said.

"Anything," I answered.

"Is he still a shit kisser?"

I laughed, loud and surprised. "Was he really that bad? So bad that you still remember?"

"Awful," Ankh said. "It was embarrassing, really. I almost offered to give him lessons."

"He's improved a little since then," I said, patting Ankh's cheek.

"Good," he said. "Nothing but the best for you."

I snuggled closer to Ankh, leaning heavily against him as his hand rubbed small circles on my arm. With my toes in the clear water of Elkin Lake, and the sun shining above, it was easy to let my eyes flicker closed and drift off.

I woke up in bed in my cabin, with a sense of completion and warmth settled deep inside me. Mal was on his side facing me, already awake, watching me with love in his rich brown eyes.

"You look happy," he said, low and adoring. "Good dreams?"

"Very good," I said. I reached out and tugged Mal closer, rolling onto my back so his body covered mine. "Waking up with you only makes it better."

He smiled, and then kissed me, slow and deep.

I was so in love with Mal—and I was in love with Ankh, too. This was the next chapter of my life, and now I knew, deep in my soul and without any doubts, that Ankh was happy for us.

We'd continue to lead this club together. We'd keep being the port in the storm for the club—the same way Mal had become mine.

"Love you," I murmured into the kiss. "So much."

"Love you, too," Mal said. "I told Dante we'd meet him at the clubhouse and help him make a brunch for everybody, since there's nothing on the schedule today. How's that sound?"

My heart swelled with love as I tugged him in for one more kiss. "Never heard anything better."

Printed in Great Britain
by Amazon